495

I, Putin

I, *Putin* is a work of fiction loosely inspired by the life of a Russian president. His wife,
children, parents, staff and prominent members of his administrations, including those
in the Russian navy and their families, are recognizable. The American president, his
administration and wife, the Estonian president and certain Russian businessmen are
recognizable. All other characters in the novel are products of the author's imagination, as
are the incidents concerning them.

ISBN: 0-6156-0252-5
ISBN-13: 978-0-615-60252-3

I, Putin

a novel by

Jennifer Ciotta

Pencey X Publishing
New York
2012

Dedication

Dedicated To
The Real Vladimir Vladimirovich Putin
&
In Memory Of
The 118 Sailors of the *Kursk*

Acknowledgements

I would like to acknowledge the following people for their contributions to this novel:

Michael Neff of the Algonkian Conferences, for his unwavering belief in this project and always invaluable advice.

NYU professors Bella Mirabella, Lauren Kaminsky, Steven Rinehart and Yanni Kotsonis for advising me in matters of Russian history/politics and creative writing.

James Simmons, judo master, for helping me explore the depths of the sport.

Ramsey Flynn, author of *Cry from the Deep*, my number one resource when researching the *Kursk* disaster.

Tatyana, my dear friend, for advising me on all matters Russian and her immense support.

My parents, Donald and Mary Jo, for encouraging my love of books and storytelling.

James, my partner, for serving as my rock when I was close to giving up, and most importantly, for serving as one of the few people who believed in this book.

Gosha snaps the belt onto the body of his dead mother. His family is not religious, but he's researched Orthodox rituals for this moment. The belt will protect Mama from evil, allowing her soul to float to heaven. A tear trickles down his cheek as he looks at her chest. It is half full. He tried to convince her to get reconstructive surgery, but she'd refused it, saying it was too expensive for a poor Russian like herself. She said she didn't want to waste money on a new breast because she was going to die anyway.

The belt is Gucci. Gosha had stolen it from his boss' gift pile of luxury items from Gucci, Louis Vuitton, Hugo Boss and other high-end retailers. His boss wouldn't miss it. Though it is a man's belt, Gosha wants his mother to be dressed in the best protection when making her way to heaven. A Gucci belt fitted tightly against her white gown shows she is someone of importance. And she was.

He wipes away the tears and looks at his watch, realizing he has an hour left. His sister Tanya sits at the end of the bed, where their dead mother lies, and holds Mama's hardening hand and rubs her knuckles. A desolate howl causes Gosha and Tanya to look up to find…nothing. It is the wind barreling against the old window pane.

"I'll leave the room so you can say goodbye. I already said mine before you came," says Tanya.

Gosha takes rubles out of his pocket. He places them in his mother's palm and closes her stiff fingers around them. This will pay for her way to heaven. Close to her, he smells her most expensive, imported perfume. Gardenias. She loved those white flowers, a rare treat whenever she saw them. He leans in closer.

"Mama, I'm sorry I can't take you to the morgue, but I have to get back to work. I chose a nice resting place for you, I hope you'll like it. It's the best I could find. As you know, I couldn't ask my boss for the favor of burying you in the best cemetery in St. Petersburg, but this is a small step below. I know Russians don't ever say this to each other, but Mama, I love you."

Tanya enters the room and reaches out to hold his hand. They turn into children, sobbing and hugging, looking to each other for comfort. They are all they have left.

After several minutes, Gosha wipes his face and exits the apartment. He knocks on the neighbor's door. A burly man holding a beer answers.

"What?"

"Can you help me carry my mother to the taxi waiting downstairs?"

The man nods.

They enter the room and the neighbor's eyes widen. He grips the neck of the beer bottle.

"She's dead?"

"Yes."

"You want me to carry a dead woman down the stairs?"

"Yes."

"I hope you're taking her to the morgue first."

"Of course. I'll grab up top and you grab her feet. Please hurry, I have to get back to work."

The man gives him a look of confusion, but places the bottle on the entry table. As they carry her down the cement stairs, Gosha tears up again but resists a good cry. Once outside he explains the situation to the taxi driver and tries to fold Mama in the trunk. The driver refuses to have to remove a dead body from his trunk in front everyone at the hospital. So they prop her up like a person in the backseat next to Tanya. Gosha closes the door. He watches the taxi drive off. Mama's dyed blond head bobs against the seat.

Another glance at his watch confirms that he has ten minutes until the press conference, which is right around the corner. He arranged it like so, because his boss thinks he's running errands. Gosha was afraid to tell him about Mama's death. Personal business is not allowed in his line of work. In fact, Gosha heard that when the President's father died, he only left the Kremlin for a few hours.

Working for The Man

Gosha Golubev is the personal aide of President Vladimir Putin. The month is March and the year is 2012. He started working for Putin in 2000, when he was first president. Then he was prime minster. And now he's president again. It's been twelve years with Putin. They've seen everything together: September 11, Beslan, terrorist attacks, oil domination. Many of Putin's colleagues—even a few of his old KGB friends—have been thrown out of the Kremlin like drunkards from a bar, but Gosha has stayed because he proved his loyalty a long time ago, in the first few months of Putin's presidency. Or at least that's what Gosha thinks.

The confusing part isn't how the boy lasted, but how he came to be hired. Even Gosha himself has no idea and asking Putin would be out of the question. Plus, Gosha doesn't want to know. He's sure the explanation isn't flattering.

He stands behind Putin, but to the left, out of the way as the media congratulates him on his reelection. This press conference is normal as reporters pamper their leader with good angles and easy questions to which Putin responds with twelve years worth of confidence. He owns Russia and he knows it. Gosha smiles. He wishes he had the confidence of his boss who sets the subservient mood of the room and plays to the cameras. After all these years, Gosha is still blinded by the purple flashes.

"Gospodin Putin, do you foresee the building of a pipeline through Siberia?"

Shoulders back and deadpan look in his eyes, Putin answers, "Yes. It will be built by 2014."

"Will the oil be distributed by ExxonMobil?"

"No. We will have full control of it. It will be distributed by us."

"Distributed by Lukoil, you mean?"

"Yes."

"But, Gospodin Putin, the Americans won't buy Lukoil if it's Russian-based."

"You are misinformed. The Americans have been buying Lukoil for years. They will buy anything as long as it fills up their big trucks."

The reporters laugh.

"Vladimir Vladimirovich, now that you're reelected, what will be your policy toward Iran and how will you work with the US if you develop a stronger relationship with Iran—"

Gosha tunes out, his mind mulling over why he was hired in the first place. He thinks back to the day of his job interview at the Kremlin.

On a whim, Gosha had filled out an application. Of course, there was no way he'd be asked to interview. So he waited for a rejection letter to arrive by post. What came instead was a phone call in the middle of the afternoon as he walked out of his history class at St. Petersburg University. A man from the Kremlin said, "We'd like you to come for an interview next week."

Gosha stared at the phone. An imaginary hand reached into the back of his throat and yanked a response out of his vocal cords.

"Okay."

The evening he left for Moscow, Mama kissed him goodbye. The kiss slid off his cold cheek and he boarded the train to the capital. All night he spooned his small suitcase, listening to the horse-like snores of men who fell asleep clutching empty vodka bottles.

With the burst of morning sun, the train rolled into Moscow, and two stops later, Gosha entered the heart of Russia.

For the first time, Red Square rumbled like a Soviet tank into his eyes. He'd only seen it on television at New Year's when the President addressed the nation. Now the Spasskaya Tower loomed overhead, a symbol of power that brought forth the hopes and dreams of the Russian people. His chest fell in relief. He was focused on the hope, not the sweltering weather or the group of perfumed, high-heeled women rushing by him in haughty strides. He tripped on a cobblestone and lost his balance, but quickly recovered.

In the massive space of Red Square, mafia types strutted, a gun tucked between their shirt and pants. Unkempt children barraged Japanese tourists, screaming insults until the Asians handed over some rubles. Across the Square, GUM, the State Department Store once flooded with the bread lines of the Soviet Union, now welcomed anyone with a gold card through its majestic, arched entryway.

And then he saw it.

Gosha felt as if the Kremlin would fall on him like a giant stone pillar, crushing him to a permanent shadow. Politicians, military leaders and cosmonauts surrounded him as he walked through Red Square, moving towards it. The ashes of their dead bodies echoed in the walls. Gosha gulped. Under these cobblestones stirred spirits from the mass graves of fallen Bolsheviks—the youngest only fourteen years of age or seven years younger than he.

But there was no time to stop and gawk.

He walked to the guard at the Spasskaya Tower entrance, but then slowed because, much to his surprise, there was no line. He assumed he'd be one of many, a long queue of those to be interviewed.

The guard stood in front of the wooden door, observing Gosha's every movement. His cast iron face, like those in the stodgy paintings of old Soviet leaders, chilled him like a Siberian winter. Gosha had expected such a sight, of course, but he found it hard to suppress a growing dread.

When the guard asked, he handed over his passport, official documents and interview letter. He looked over everything then cursed under his breath, something that sounded to Gosha like *sykin sin*, son of a bitch, but Gosha pretended he had not heard. The guard then sliced his hand through the air in the direction of the door, a signal for Gosha to move as quickly as possible on to the next security station.

The arched wooden door opened, a disappointment to Gosha, who had expected enormous golden doors entering into a dark place. A hand grabbed him and pulled him into the foyer. The next thing he knew, a flurry of metal detectors poked and prodded. Guards patted him down, rummaged through his suitcase and questioned him. A lone guard took him by the arm, fingers biting through Gosha's sleeve into his flesh. He escorted him down a long, dark hallway, their shoes echoing off the pristine marble floor and down the corridor with a sound like wooden canes smacking down hard on a man's back. Gosha thought of an old KGB interrogation room. Dank and dim. A lone light bulb hanging from the ceiling by a thin string. The funnel where a prisoner placed his head to be shot through the wall. He began to shake, and the guard gripped his arm harder and mumbled something, a word Gosha could have sworn was *ubl-oo-dock*, nasty scum.

In the distance, at the end of the dark corridor, he saw an open door. A secret service man in a dark suit and earpiece stood on either side. Once they arrived before the two men, the guard let go of the boy's arm and shoved him through the doorway. In the bleak office, the guard forced a smile of steel-black teeth and shoved him once more toward a vacant chair, the only chair in the room. Gosha stumbled backwards and sat. Everything happened so fast, he hadn't noticed the secretary perched behind a desk in the corner. She was so ancient, wrinkles mapped out her face. Her emerald eyes were not warm like a loving grandmother. The upturned corners of her mouth were about to form an appropriate welcome until the door behind her creaked open then shut. The remnants of an almost smile disappeared, no longer available to assuage Gosha's tension.

She stared at the boy, her face devoid of any warmth, and said, "Who are you?"

"I—I have an appointment. A—A personal aide interview."

She looked into her ledger. A single finger slid down the paper until it stopped.

"Yes. You."

"Y—Yes. I'm Gosha."

"You're Gosha."

"That's me."

"Good for you."

She snapped the ledger shut.

Gosha jumped.

"Get your CV ready. You will be called in very soon."

He reached into the pocket of his suitcase and pulled out his CV. The sweat from his palms poured onto the paper. He was barely able to type more than a page because his professional experience didn't extend beyond the grocery store and a semester-long assistant position at university. He spent most of his time photocopying and scanning copyrighted materials onto the professors' websites and then begging for permission via email to use more copyrights. Gosha wrote exactly what he did, like an idiot, cursing himself in his mind, thinking of what a dumb decision it was to be honest.

He wiped his palms on the fabric of his suit jacket and rested them on his lap. His CV had smear marks due to excessive sweating so he shoved it back into the pocket of his suitcase and pulled out a fresh one. A deep breath ensued. The air passing through his lungs down to his chest calmed him. The President wasn't interviewing him; it was just an advisor, the man who had called him. He would go in there, be unimpressive and have a story to tell his phantom children. That was all Gosha wanted, a good story. A lifetime of hardly dating, studying all the time to keep up with his classmates and trying to earn some extra money to add to the family finances—this was what Gosha was used to. Not some fancy office with gold trim around the doors and on the walls, or the chair he was sitting on, probably on loan from the Hermitage. It was all relative. In this new world, relativity swallowed him up and he was soon to be spat out.

The phone bleated. The unfriendly secretary picked up the receiver and listened. She nodded then hung up. Her eyes shot to Gosha and her pink-frosted mouth opened wide as if she was about to say something. Then it closed. Finally, she opened it again and words came out.

"Gospodin Putin is ready for you. I will bring you in now."

Gosha's mouth dried instantly, as if he had swallowed a gust of wind off the steppes, a dustbowl sucking the moisture out of him. He whispered, "I thought…I was going to interview with Gospodin Putin's advisor?"

"Vladimir Vladimirovich likes to interview prospective aides himself."

She opened the door as Gosha slowly rose from his chair, desperately wanting to extend time as long as he possibly could. He told himself, *Go in there. You have to. Move. Just move!* He grasped the handle of his suitcase and began to walk while his breath quickened. *Just move.* Sweat flowed from a new area on his body, his forehead. *Move, dammit!* As he passed through the doorway, he looked back at the empty chair. The secretary cleared her throat, giving him a strange look. Gosha turned around and kept walking forward.

The Interview

After three hours of standing on his feet at the press conference, Gosha's back kills. He rubs his lumbar area. Putin rattles on about the economy and how he expects it to prevail, especially since Russia no longer wastes money by converting to US dollars when trading with China. He looks at the President's face. There are deep wrinkles and his hairline recedes to that of an old man. He isn't the picture of youth he was when Gosha first met him at his job interview.

The head of Gospodin Putin was bent over a stack of papers while his hand scribbled a signature. Gosha assumed the President hadn't noticed when he entered the room—an office as large as a two bedroom flat in the most luxurious part of Piter. He stood and shuffled his feet on the Oriental carpet then coughed. Gospodin Putin did not raise his head. Gosha examined the blond hair, thinning out from middle to front, the combed sections, parted perfectly like a Soviet schoolboy. Putin's fingers gripped the pen as he signed furiously. His fingernails were trimmed to the precise length of being comfortable. He was so small in stature, a child sitting behind his father's desk.

"Sit."

Gosha assumed he heard correctly so he backpedaled and sat in another chair, another priceless piece of art.

Putin stopped the frenzy of signing and looked up. Pancake makeup gave his face a distorted orange glow, all of his hard features washed out onto a cakey surface. Gosha had not expected such a thing. Perhaps he just finished a television interview or was about to attend one. His tie was perfectly knotted around his collar, covering his slim neck, void of the usual businessman's roll of fat. He smelled of expensive cologne, a hint of musk, strong enough to be noticed in a room full of sycophants, warning them to keep in their places, yet light enough to convince his female supporters of his harmlessness.

A chill ran down Gosha's spine as the infamous stare bored through his pupils to every bone in his body. Putin laid his pen on the desk and folded his arms into a praying position with fingers interlaced. He stared. For an eternity. Yet in real time, it was about ten seconds. *Should I look away?* Gosha took a sudden interest in a Yeltsin bobble head on Putin's desk and concentrated on its squinty grin.

"Give me your CV."

Gosha rushed to the desk and handed it to him, nearly knocking over the priceless chair from getting up so fast. He returned to his seat.

Putin's eyes flashed over it in a matter of seconds, not the full reading Gosha had expected, but at least it saved him the humiliation of skimming the words "photocopying" and "request by email."

"What does this mean?" Putin asked, as the steel blue irises penetrated the boy's.

Gosha opened his arid mouth. "E—excuse me, Gospodin Putin?"

"You are inexperienced."

"Y—yes. I am."

Putin said nothing in response. His eyes returned to the paper.

"Why do you want to be my personal aide?"

Instead of answering the question, Gosha had the urge to wipe the sides of his mouth with his thumb and forefinger. Crust had settled there, but he stopped himself, figuring it was inappropriate to do in front of the President.

"I think I'd be a good personal aide for you, Vladimir Vladimirovich. I have worked with other superiors such as my professors and even the Dean at university. I feel that I can predict and access the needs of others and help them achieve their goals."

It popped out of his mouth in a shaky, uncontrolled voice that lilted like a school boy who had hit puberty. Gosha had no idea how scanning a document into a computer could do all this, especially since the professors hardly ever spoke to him. How had he performed the magic of turning menial work into making dreams come true?

No reaction, Putin continued to browse the CV. Gosha prepared himself for a question about his job or education experience.

"Anything else?"

He couldn't fool this man. The tone in his voice conveyed to Gosha this was his last chance. It better be good and it better be the truth.

"G—Gospodin Putin, I know I'm not very experienced. Of course, you can see that from my CV. I have a feeling you don't understand why your advisor chose me and honestly, I have no idea either. But I got the call and I'm here and ready to work for the country I love. I'm sorry but that's all I have."

Putin looked up from the paper and stared at Gosha again, but this time, he stared with piercing curiosity, not ice. The curiosity softened his eyes into an ocean of calm water. Gosha felt he could swim in them until they shifted to the floor. A rat scurried across the carpet and disappeared under a bookshelf. Then in a blink, the flat countenance reappeared on Putin's face, bored and uninterested, exactly as the interview had started.

"You may leave."

"It was an honor to meet you, Gospodin Putin," Gosha said as he swiped his suitcase and rushed out of the office with intense speed.

Safe in the hallway, he reached up to wipe the sides of his mouth. But a new guard grabbed him by the arm and escorted him back down the corridor.

That wasn't so bad.

Two days later he received the phone call. And after witnessing all the reactions of his friends, family and acquaintances, he knew a miracle had occurred, and he didn't know how. He came from a poor family, thus nepotism was not a factor; in fact, the closest his immediate family had come to the Kremlin was on a planned summer vacation when Gosha was nine. His mother saved up all year long for a trip to Moscow, including tours, meals, train tickets and a five-night hostel stay. Yet the trip never happened because a few days before his grandmother had fallen ill.

The story of his life. Someone he loves, usually a woman, gets sick and dies. Gosha doesn't want to remember anymore. It's been a sad enough day already, his mother dying. He left his sister crying in the taxi as it drove away from the apartment building. Now, he can only comfort her by phone because he won't have the time to visit. And the President will return to Moscow later today.

"Thank you for coming everyone. Your tough questions are appreciated. I serve the Russian people, and I appreciate that you hold me to a high standard."

Putin steps off the platform and walks off stage. Flashes and reporters follow him, blurting out questions and congratulations. Out in the parking lot, he strides to the car in his signature thug-like walk. Gosha closes the limo door for him and then goes around to the other side and gets in. In his hand is his mobile, which is always ready to take notes, call someone at Putin's request, or text or email someone, since the President refuses to engage in technology.

As the car takes off, he turns to Gosha. "Read me my schedule for today."

"Yes, Gospodin Putin. Let me pull it up on my phone."

He clicks the buttons on his mobile.

"Right now, you have a lunch with the mayor of Piter. Then you have a public relations visit to a judo tournament, where you'll make an appearance for approximately twenty minutes. After that, you'll board a private plane back to Moscow. I've scheduled an early dinner with your wife."

"Why?"

Gosha stays silent.

Putin responds to his own question. "To keep up appearances."

"Yes, Vladimir Vladimirovich…But some good news, Masha will be there."

"My daughter is here from the US?"

"Yes."

"When did she arrive?"

"She will arrive in a few hours."

"Make sure there's a gift waiting for her. Whatever she prefers."

"Of course, that's already been taken care of."

"And get my wife a gift too."

"Of course. I'll run to Hermes and pick her up a handbag."

"Don't waste money. Just pick from the freebie pile. It's familiar to you since you already do that for yourself. I hope you enjoyed the Gucci belt this morning."

Gosha freezes. His face flushes as he turns away from the President.

"Sixteen years in the KGB and you think I can't figure out if someone took a belt?"

Gosha's insides knot like an American hot pretzel, which he'd eaten on his last trip to New York.

"And I also know your 'errand' was your dead mother."

The boy drops his phone on the car floor. As he reaches to pick it up, he hears: "Personal business should not interfere with your work. You were almost late to the press conference."

"Yes, Gospodin Putin."

Putin wasn't always so cold and stoic. He had feelings once, a long way back in the first few months of his original presidential term. Then something happened. And it changed Putin into the person he is today.

Gosha prefers to remember those times and keep them close in his mind. He knows his boss has a human side, since he makes sure Masha has a present upon her arrival.

"And what's going on with the memoirs?"

Gosha focuses on his boss' voice. "The publisher would like to read the first draft of your memoirs by June, if possible. They'd like to publish it right after you become president again."

"I will dictate them to you. And you will type them up."

Gosha silently thanks the Universe, since his boss' handwriting is illegible.

"Yes, Gospodin Putin."

"But that's something we'll work on at a later time. Right now, I need to focus on my prime minister duties and upcoming inauguration. We'll work on the book in between."

Gosha taps away on his phone, writing back to the senior editor at the publishing house that, yes, the memoirs should be ready by June. He wonders what the President is going to say. Would he edit himself or be forthright with his audience? Would he play the hero, like always, or display himself as a regular person, which he was, before becoming involved in politics. His appeal to ordinary Russians is the fact he came from nothing, like them. He can be the billionaire, self-declared authoritarian he is now, or he can be himself. Which one would he choose?

Dinner

In the outskirts of Moscow, back at the Putin villa, she stomps through the doorway, a mobile attached to her ear. Her designer boots clack against the marble floor, signaling Mariya Vladimirovna Putina's arrival. She unwraps herself from the long black coat and hands it to the help, nodding in thank you. The boots clack again, rounding the corner to Putin's office, where Gosha pores over paperwork.

The office door creaks. Mariya, informally known as Masha, steps inside and asks, "Where is my father?"

Gosha turns around to the tall, blond beauty. A face like her father's, but feminine. The aqua eyes match the paisley in her silk scarf. Her skirt falls to her knees, which her father will approve of. He dislikes when she wears anything short or too tight, as she used to do as a teenager.

"He's swimming."

"Okay. I'll be out here in the living room. We're all going out to dinner? Still keeping up appearances?"

"Yes."

Gosha chooses to make polite conversation with her as he always tries to do. "How is New York?"

"Cold."

"How are your studies going?"

"The same."

"You must miss Moscow."

"Sometimes, but there are enough Russians in New York to feel at home. And most of them have no idea who I am, so that's nice."

With that, she leaves the room and marches down the hallway. Gosha shakes his head and returns to the paperwork. As he continues to read through the incomprehensible documents, he thinks that Masha acts like a child, taking for granted that both of her parents are still alive. *I'm an orphan.* Mama is dead, and his father, well, who knows where he is.

"Tell my daughter we'll leave for dinner in thirty minutes."

He hadn't heard Putin enter the room, but as he turns around, he sees his boss in a spa robe, wiping his head with a towel from the indoor swimming pool's bathroom. Then he walks out.

"Yes, Gospodin Putin."

If that were his sister Tanya, he'd merely open the door and scream to her. But this is work and it's Masha Putina, and even though he's been with the family for twelve years, he's nowhere near becoming a friend or family member. He's simply a servant, a maid in the form of paperwork, scheduling and fetching.

Gosha leaves the room, by accident stepping on several sheets of paper. He glances at them and sees that he hasn't left any shoe marks. Down the hallway, Masha and her father embrace. It is a sweet, generous hug for Putin, who actually does love his daughters. To the outside world, they are hidden, even on the Internet. Masha leads a quiet life as a graduate student in New York, while her younger sister Katya lives in a small German town with a boyfriend and German shepherd. This is what Putin wanted for both of them, a life of peace and quiet with the ability to fulfill their dreams and have unlimited access to money. He's created this life for them, and they may be grateful on some level, but to Gosha, they are spoiled.

Instead, Gosha gave most of his salary to his mother, though he didn't mind. It paid her hospital bills and provided her the ability to live in a two-bedroom apartment in the nice part of Piter with his sister Tanya. The apartment is now Tanya's, and it is expensive for her salary, so Gosha will once again give a portion of his own salary to her. Tanya has a job as an accountant, but she certainly can't afford a two-bedroom by herself and now is not the time to ask her to move. Gosha would like her to get married soon, since he loves his sister, but does not want to financially support her for the rest of her life. It's too much. Everyone else around him has dreams, and many have lived them out, especially the Putins, but for Gosha, his ultimate dream is to retrieve his life. Right now, his life is Vladimir Putin's life. In essence, he's a shadow.

One day, he will be a person. He holds onto this dream like glue sticking to paper. He'll date, he'll go to the movies, he'll have a wife and kids and he'll live...he'll live in the United States! California, where it's sunny and warm and the Americans are friendlier than the Russians. Where the imported palm tree fronds sway in the breeze coming off the salty ocean. He can almost smell the salt, feel the sun on his pale, Russian face—

"What are you doing?"

Putin's voice interrupts his reverie. Gosha has been staring at the wall, smiling.

He turns around to Masha and his boss, "Dinner is in thirty minutes." And he walks away, back to the office to bury himself in paperwork. The Putins stare after him.

At the restaurant, Gosha stands next to the wall, in earshot of the Putins' dinner. He has yet to be invited to sit with them.

"Mashenka, how is New York?"

"Cold."

"How are your studies?"

"The same."

"Masha, give us more than that. After all, we're paying for your fancy New York apartment and fancy New York graduate school."

"No, Mama. Papa is paying."

Lyudmila Aleksandrovna Putina puts her fork on her plate. Gosha's stomach sinks and he braces for a fight.

"Your father's money is my money too."

"What do you do for it?"

Lyuda grabs her champagne flute and drinks.

"You should not speak that way to your mother. You're a woman in your twenties. You should show more respect than that."

"Yes, Papa."

"Fine, let's continue our meal. Masha, I'd like to hear about your graduate studies."

She talks about her classes, the professors and how well she's done on tests. She criticizes American academia, citing how easy the exams and papers are. But the one thing she doesn't like is all the strict rules about referencing sources. In Russia, it's easier to plagiarize.

Gosha rolls his eyes. Masha used to be likeable. They were never friends, but she was an approachable teenager and a good source of entertainment when she annoyed her father, but now she acts harsh and guarded. She's turning into her father and turning against her mother. Gosha knows it saddens Lyudmila Putina because of her withdrawn face the entire meal, the nibbling of meat and the avoided eye contact with her husband and daughter. They have everything: money, power and fame. But the one thing they're lacking is each other, and to Gosha, that's a waste of a perfectly good dinner.

After Dinner

Putin retires to his office, his daughter to her bedroom and his wife to her apartment in Red Square. Gosha is ready to leave for the night, to retire to his hovel right outside the Kremlin. He bundles himself in a wool scarf and black coat. As he yanks his gloves from his pockets, Putin calls his name. Gosha sighs. He wanted to be out of there before 23.00, so he could kick back with a beer and watch some television on his lumpy futon.

"Yes, Gospodin Putin," he says, while trudging back to the office.

"Let's start on the memoirs. I'm ready."

He takes off his coat and unwraps the scarf. Putin sits by the empty fireplace, holding a snifter of cognac. It's a small amount, enough to relax him and show he's Russian. Gosha sits down in the chair opposite him and takes out his mobile. He sets it to record and places it on the table between them.

"Okay, Gospodin Putin. Where would you like to start?"

"My childhood."

"Go ahead. It's recording."

St. Petersburg 1962

In my childhood, the rats were my friends.

My parents were not aware but I fed them every day after school. If my mother and father had known I was squandering food for my rodent friends Krushy and Peter when food itself was scarce, I would've been reprimanded, so I kept it to myself. The first time I brought dinner to the rats, they scurried over to me as if they already knew what was coming. I liked the sound of their feet pattering across the cement and the sight of their pink noses twitching at the scent of meat. Dropping the gristly beef on the floor, I would back away as they pounced on it with glee and gorged on their wet, soggy meal. Meanwhile, my mouth would start to water and my stomach would growl as I'd think to myself, the rats dined better than the people in my country.

They looked hungry when I'd come home every day, hovering in the darkness under the stairwell of my apartment building's lobby. I'd begun this ritual one day at school lunch by stuffing the meat from my goulash into my coat pocket. They kept getting thinner and thinner, so I dedicated myself to making them healthier, stronger.

The goulash in my pocket stunk all day long, which caused my classmates to sniff at the area around me, asking, "Vladimir Putin, is that you that stinks?" Another boy added, "Goulash Pants—his new nickname—Goulash Pants." A third said, "What about Mr. Goulash Pants?" In the end I was called "Goulash Pants," but I didn't care; they weren't my friends. I hadn't any of those. And when they taunted me from then on, my hand would close around the slimy beef, thinking, I HATE YOU.

On weekdays, I left my apartment building at seven, walking the streets of Piter to go to school. I looked down into the canals at the murky water, which did not stir. Sailors strolled by in their navy uniforms and I thought to myself, a sailor's life is the best, waking up early, walking in peace along the street, no one bothering you.

I'll never forget one morning in particular. Ten minutes into my walk, I rounded the corner of the Church of the Savior on Blood. I grew panicked and looked from left to right. I saw no one and continued walking. Then I heard several footsteps from behind me. I walked faster, soon jogging then trying to run. Suddenly someone grabbed me and wrapped his thick fingers around my neck. Another pair of hands gripped my bony triceps while my books clattered on the pavement. I started to scream but a fist came out of nowhere and smashed into my cheekbone as a knee jabbed me in the groin. I doubled over, fell to the ground and began to wheeze. They gave up when the wheezing began. They released me and ran off in another direction.

I lifted my head and saw the golden onion dome of the Church, the sun reflecting off it, making it appear more gold and majestic. I wanted to be on top of that dome, high in the sky so no one could get to me. I would sit up there and look out over all of Piter like a king on his throne. The wind would lift me up and guide me over my kingdom. At that moment, it sounded nice and I smiled through the pain in my face, pushing myself off the ground and gathering my books. I continued on my way to school—bruised, scraped, bleeding—and went to class after class, yet the teachers never questioned my appearance, which was routine. They probably assumed it was a family matter, that my father was an alcoholic. Other boys came to school with black eyes and welts on a regular basis. I wasn't anyone special.

That was school in the Soviet Union. The teachers looked the other way at broken down children. Because we were all broken down. Going to school was like going from grey to grey, concrete to concrete, boring to boring. Teachers recited from textbooks and we memorized the information and regurgitated it back on tests. Science experiments, class trips, contest prizes didn't exist. Who had the money? The first day of school was the most interesting—though not that interesting at all—with The First Bell ceremony. Parents gave us flowers and adored the first form children as they took their initial steps onto the school grounds. We handed the young ones their first books and led them into the school, as a bugle sounded and Pioneer and Komsomol banners waved in the crowd.

"What about your home life, Gospodin Putin? Can you expand on that?" asks Gosha.

"Don't interrupt me."

Putin clears his throat and continues.

Mama, Papa and I lived in a communal flat with two other families. There was ours then a second family which consisted of an old Jewish couple and their thirty-year-old daughter. The third family was a single mother with a set of twin babies. It was a one bedroom apartment, and a hanging rug divided the bedroom. One half belonged to us with my mother and father sharing a bed and I had a cot. On the other side of the room, the Jewish couple and daughter had the same setup. We gave the mother and her babies the living room because they cried and screamed. The Jews were quiet, only requesting the kitchen table on Friday nights for Sabbath dinner.

Even though we had a small kitchen without hot water or an oven, we did have a hot plate. There was no washroom or toilet inside the apartment; the three bottom floors shared one with no tub and a rotting toilet. My father carved a toilet seat from some extra wood at my grandmother's *dacha*, summer cottage, sandpapering it until it was smooth to sit on. My mother, father and I would bring it to the communal toilet with us and carefully place it on the top of the ice cold rim. Meanwhile, the moldy government toilet seat leaned against the asbestos wall.

The walls were very thin in our *khrushchoby*, our garbage dump slum. As I climbed the stairs, I could hear my neighbors fighting floors above me. Every word reverberated. I heard drunken fights, loud sex, the practicing of instruments and babies wailing. It was noisy day and night. I learned to fall asleep amidst the chaos.

Each day when I came home from school, I unlocked the front door and entered our apartment to find Liliya—that was her name—smoking a cigarette in the living room. Along with that insufferable habit, the apartment stunk because she rarely changed her babies' diapers. They sat in their own filth by the balcony door and played with toy blocks the old Jewish woman, Riva, had given them. Liliya, in her dingy stretched-out nightgown that failed to cover her chest, didn't look up or say hi as cigarette smoke billowed around her craggy face. Though one breast was exposed, she wasn't anything to look at—even for a young boy. It was a saggy, wrinkled piece of flesh.

I put my books down on the kitchen table and went to our side of the bedroom. I lay down on the bed and looked up at the ceiling. This hour before people came home from their jobs as industrial workers, doctors, telephone operators, teachers and postal workers was my alone time. Despite the dirty diapers, the suffocating smoke and the noise from several neighbors, I closed my eyes and let my mind wander. I dreamt of having a house, the kind of house that I had seen in a movie about the West a few months before. The Soviet government had banned the film but I snuck in the back of an underground theater to see it. I'd overheard the other boys in my class talk about going, yet I didn't have the money for a ticket. So when the movie began, I slipped past the guards whose eyes were glued to the screen, risking the punishment of a serious beating.

I hid behind a long curtain and watched images of small farmhouses fill the screen. Each family owned one, and on the inside, the mother and father shared a bedroom while the children had separate bedrooms. There was indoor plumbing with running water of both hot and cold that flowed from the faucet in a clear stream, not the brown guck that came out of ours. The toilet sat perched with a gleaming seat, made of expensive porcelain or some other material I could hardly imagine. The voiceover said:

"This is how the Scandinavians live."

Each had a small garden where they grew their own vegetables. On the screen, a man picked a red tomato, the color of fresh blood, showed it to the camera and took a loud bite. Juice dribbled down his chin.

We all gasped.

This was not our life. Our life was waiting in line for bread and rough toilet paper. I'd never experienced biting into a fresh vegetable because our stores were vacant most of the time, and when they had fruit, it was rotting and rationed out to a lucky few.

I left the theater immediately after seeing the tomato. It was too overwhelming. I'd found out shortly after that the Soviet police had raided the movie house. They incarcerated the entire audience and the guards. They lined up the movie house owners against a wall and shot them in the head. When I heard the news, I breathed a sigh of relief for escaping.

I looked up at the cracks in the bedroom ceiling and thought of the better life that was out there. Even at my young age, I knew communism wasn't working, not the way it should. Why were we living in such squalor if my father was a respected member of the Communist Party? I didn't understand why my toolmaker father and janitor mother worked so long and so hard to take care of people like Liliya, a woman who was capable of working yet received a small assistance from the state for being a single mother. My father would say, "That lazy bitch gets money from the state because her husband left her? If only the state met her, it would do the same thing."

He was especially bitter because he was a retired military man who had nearly lost his leg to a battlefield explosion, yet collected no compensation from the state. So he hated Liliya. He could turn her in—and he knew the Jewish family would vouch for him—but there were consequences. We'd heard of problem tenants being taken in the middle of the night and shipped off to hard labor in Siberia. The babies would surely die on the train ride over and Papa had nothing against them. Liliya would wither and die not long after her babies on that train ride. My father couldn't have that on his conscience so he never alerted the authorities.

Liliya scampered across the living room floor. A dresser drawer squealed open and banged shut. The dirty diaper smell dissipated as water flowed from the faucet into the kitchen sink. Liliya was probably washing her face and running a brush through her hair, getting dressed and applying a little lipstick as well, the kind bought on the black market. She smacked her lips.

I knew she did all this in preparation for when my father came home. She wasn't dumb. She was lazy, but not dumb. Instead, she was well aware of Papa's contempt for her and didn't want to aggravate the uncomfortable living situation further. Her solution was to pretend like she'd put in a full day's work taking care of the babies.

My father's keys rattled in the front door. I came out of the bedroom to greet him. His heavy boots hit the floor as Liliya wrapped her babies in clothes and headed out to the park. My father scowled at her as she swept past him with a child in each arm. He knew that she sat around all day, but at least she left him in peace for a few hours.

He looked at me, said hello then retreated to the bedroom to take a nap. I sat on the end of Liliya's bed and stared out the balcony door, similar to her minus the cigarette and babies. Across the street was a grey building of Soviet bloc housing. Dust and dirt flew up into the sky as *babooshki*, Russian grannies, beat rugs out on their balconies. Stray cats swarmed around below, mewing and arching their backs, since someone had probably thrown a few fish bones on the ground or maybe they were in heat. A man lifted another man into a dumpster on the side of the building. He came out empty-handed, shrugged at his friend and they walked to the next apartment complex in search of food or anything else of use.

At that moment, I remembered the words my mother often told me when she read the melancholy in my eyes.

"These are hard times, Volodya. We have to make opportunities for ourselves. We have to take control of our destinies."

Judo

Putin sits back in the plush chair. He taps his finger on the cognac snifter. Gosha hopes he is done with his memoirs for tonight. The one thing that annoys him about his boss is that he's a night owl. This man will stay up until one or two in the morning doing mundane work things, like reading over legislation or viewing video of the week's news to ensure he's portrayed in a positive or neutral light.

Gosha, however, is a morning person. He loves waking up to the fresh sunshine—when there is sunshine in Moscow—and standing in the middle of Red Square in the early morning and thinking to himself that he's made it. All of his classmates from high school and college have wives and babies and take leisurely vacations, but he's given up the last twelve years of his life to the state, which is more honorable than having someone to love. When Putin relinquishes power in 2024 (he guesses), Gosha will have saved enough money to call himself rich. He'll be 44 years old and ready to settle down. If he's rich, he can marry any gorgeous Russian woman he wants. Which is why he needs to wean Tanya off his money in the next six months. He presses pause on his mobile to stop recording and brings up his electronic notes and types: *Find Tanya a potential husband by Victory Day.* It's more than a bank holiday for him; May 9 will change his future.

"Young people never stop clicking."

"Yes, Gospodin Putin."

"I'd like to continue. Start recording."

Gosha places the mobile back on the table, but he really wants to smack it down and show his boss he's infuriated that he has to give up himself for yet another night. Instead, he listens.

When I was ten years old, my physical education teacher was the only teacher I liked. I respected Anatoly Ivanovich because he didn't favor any-one—not the bullies, the naturally athletic kids or the privileged kids. Everyone deserved a chance to prove himself in his eyes. In me, I don't know what he saw except a scrawny kid from the bad side of town.

Around my tenth birthday, Anatoly Ivanovich asked me to stay after class. I'd never been asked to stay before; only kids who had acted up during class had to stay after.

He waited until everyone left the gym.

"Volodya, I've learned of a scholarship opening. In one of the martial arts."

I looked down toward the gym floor. This was not the path I'd wanted to take—to be tortured by my bullies after school as well. They would be in advanced classes and I would be in beginner. The *volkodavs*, wolf-killing dogs, would be released on me, a defenseless wolf pup.

"Which martial art? Sambo?"

"Judo. My friend owns a judo studio and the state has given him money for new scholarship participants. As you know, the state actively supports sambo, but realizes that in international and Olympic competition, they are getting nowhere. They must switch over to judo if the Soviet Union wants to be competitive on a worldwide level."

"Why me?" It slipped out of my mouth but I had to know the answer. Why trust a scholarship to a small, skinny, average-student kid?

Anatoly Ivanovich shuffled his feet and hesitated a moment before answering. "Because, Volodya, I know you get the shit kicked out of you nearly every day by those thugs."

My face turned red.

"You need protection. You're very small—you will be small all your life—but you're very fast and athletically-inclined. And most importantly, you're not living up to your potential. I've heard many times from your teachers that they're frustrated by your laziness. They say you're smart. I think judo is the way out for you."

He stopped talking and stared at me. I assumed he wanted a decision right then and there, but for me it was a big decision to make. The training would be paid for. And my bullies would be in sambo while I was in judo so I'd avoid them altogether. I had nothing else to do everyday but go home and see Liliya's scraggly boob or hear my father snore as he took his afternoon nap. Pleasing my father would be a large part of this too, since he'd like the idea of me being able to defend myself. He had great hopes of me going into the army or following his footsteps into the navy—he'd never actually said it, but I could tell. I liked the idea of pleasing him, but I had no interest in following in his footsteps. The idea of being on the verge of a martial art uprising interested me. Sambo, a combination of judo and wrestling, couldn't go beyond the borders of the Soviet Union. Judo could.

I was taking too long.

"Vova, it's your choice. I need an answer now. Otherwise I have many other boys who will jump at this chance."

"Yes."

A week later I pulled open the door of the judo studio to see the students rolling across the mats. It reminded me of how I used to roll my body down the grassy hill at my grandparents' dacha. The students then halted and rolled back in the direction they had just come from. The air was stale and smelled of sweat and body odor. All around the room were large mirrors like in a ballet studio. A student led the exercises for the class.

The sensei watched over everything from a spot in the corner, like a stoic guard at the Kremlin gates. Small in stature but big in presence, I knew to be instantly frightened of him. And I liked it. He had all the power, in the corner, watching over the students. No one could question him in any way. No one could rise above him.

He nodded to the student leading the exercises. The boy grabbed a uniform off a chair and came over to me. "Put it on and come back out."

The first time I put on the judogi it felt like a rough bed sheet encompassing my body. I wrapped the belt around my waist and tied it. Power enveloped me like a superhero donning his cape.

Back in the studio, the boy leader lectured me on the philosophy of judo, how it meant "gentle way" in Japanese and that I must be in control at all times. It went against everything I knew, yet it comforted me somehow. He gave me books to study in order to catch up since I was starting halfway through the year. One quote in particular resonated with me: "Greatness lies not in being strong, but in the right use of strength." How I would use my newfound strength was what mattered.

After seeing enough progress, the boy leader introduced me to my sensei.

"This is Vladimir Putin."

He nodded then looked away. In my mind I accepted this reaction. He hadn't spoken to the entire class so why would he suddenly start speaking to me? I stepped on the tatami and felt a desire to impress my new sensei. Even though he wasn't watching me, I still yearned to do my best. This was a change from my regular attitude, especially when in school, since getting average marks was usually enough for me. I didn't see a need to excel beyond my limits because I had assumed I'd be in communal housing for the rest of my life. A feeling awoke in me that day though, the feeling that I could escape what I had imagined to be my destiny.

Perhaps you could call it hope.

So I devoured my judo books. Nothing could tear me apart from them. My father let me eat dinner when I wanted even though my mother protested. Family dinner was her way of sidestepping the insanity of our flat, coming together to enjoy at least twenty minutes in peace. Not allowed to bring my books to the table, I sat under the light bulb of our half of the bedroom and read. Everything finally made sense—it was as though I'd been punched in the face by an awakening. I'd been training for this all my life. All of the beatings from the bullies would make me less afraid in matches. Some of the other beginners were afraid to get hurt, we could all tell. Not me. I didn't hesitate to volunteer as a practice dummy when the more advanced students needed to hone their skills for competition. I was the person who jumped in first when trying a new throw or grappling technique.

My sensei caught on; he knew I was serious about the sport. About a year later some of the beginners had dropped out, uninterested or untalented. I renewed my scholarship for another year and kept reading my judo books as well, but never at school. I didn't want the other kids to see what I was doing, preferring to sneak up on them when the time was right. Just like the judo principle—wait and watch, then react.

Finally, my time had come to be tested. And I felt ready.

The beatings had become less. I didn't know if the bullies sensed I was becoming a new person, stronger or maybe more confident, but they had relented. They'd moved onto a new class of younger boys. At least that was what I had thought. However, they had to prove themselves, have a go at me once more for old time's sake.

These boys were experts in sambo so I knew I couldn't defend myself until I was sufficiently trained. The sensei never spoke to me unless he had to, but the boy leader said that I was very advanced for the first year. I had combined three years of judo into one, moving into the advanced group after a year of training, which surprised me. At home I put more effort into studying and grew confident in my intellect, as well as my athletic abilities. On the street I carried myself with shoulders back and abs tightened, making myself appear taller.

I hadn't competed in a formal tournament though. Little did I know my first competition would be back on the street in front of the Church with the golden dome.

I walked my normal route to school and on that day I actually whistled. It was a beautiful spring morning with birds flying in the sky. The sun felt good after a long St. Petersburg winter.

Suddenly, cold hands wrapped around my neck and choked me while another pair gripped my triceps. This time my triceps weren't bony. They were muscular. Surprised by this new development, the bully loosened his grip. This was my chance. I took hold of his hands and twisted them into an excruciating position, letting out a guttural yell. He screamed. The other boy was so frightened that his hands sprung off my neck. Before they had the chance to react, I turned around and pushed one boy to the ground. I grabbed the other and threw him down on the pavement. He landed on his back, arms failing like a hysterical baby. I picked up my books and went on my way to school, whistling softly to myself.

My first competition played out much the same way. I wasn't placed at the advanced level in tournaments to start out despite the fact I was training in an advanced class. The boy leader said my sensei wanted to start me out slowly. I didn't agree. Of course, I thought I could handle the best, since my confidence was high after defending myself against the bullies. The one boy wore wrist braces for two weeks while the other missed several days of classes due to a "bad back." I easily anticipated my competitor's moves at the first match then the second then the third. After my fourth win, I showed up late to practice thinking, "Who cares if I'm late? I'm winning for my sensei, making him and his studio look good."

He had a different view.

After that tardiness, the boy leader came up to me. "The sensei wants to speak with you."

I strolled over to him. In the rare times he asked to speak to me, I rushed over yet I didn't feel like it at that moment. He watched my every step. His cold eyes bored into mine.

"You think you good?"

I shrugged. Of course I thought I was good.

"OK. You so good, you prove good tomorrow. In advanced match. Very special competitor for you."

He smiled. I'd never seen him smile before. My skin shot up with goose bumps.

I'd watched the advanced students compete before me. Who was this special competitor? At this point I knew most of the competition from the other studios and none of them had abilities that superseded mine.

The day of the match, I bounced around like an overeager boxer. The boy leader came over to calm my nerves, and I stretched with him. We sat on the ground, the soles of our feet touching as we grabbed hands and pulled. In the bleachers my father stared at the scene in front of him while my mother smiled down on me. Then it was time to proceed to the green tatami. I stood up straight, tightened my obi and waited for my competition.

Out came a girl. A very tiny one. A practical feather compared to my frame. I looked over to my sensei who was smiling from ear to ear.

She stepped onto the mat, bowing to me. In return, I bowed to her, stunned that I had to fight this little girl. I'd never competed against a female before. I didn't want to hurt her fragile bones or pretty face. On the outside my face remained stern, but on the inside I laughed.

The referee yelled, Hajime! Before I could react, the little thing darted at me, grabbing my left elbow and my right shoulder and pounding me belly up onto the mat. I reached for the shoulders of her kimono but before I could latch on, she flipped me on my stomach in one motion, wrapping her piercing fingers around my head. I squirmed to get her off of me, but I couldn't. Then making an amateur mistake, I slipped my arm out from underneath her. She clamped on, straightening out the arm then twisting the wrist. The bones snapped as I let out a cry of torture.

The referee didn't call time nor was the girl done with me. The match went on for another excruciating minute as she grabbed me off the tatami and threw me down in another spot, jumping on top of me, her pointy elbows and body weight pushing down on my ribs. Two more snaps. My ribs were broken.

For her final move, she went in for a choke hold, digging her long nails into my neck. My breath shortened as my eyes bulged. I smelled the body odor embedded in the mat. The referee declared her the winner and ended the match. I hobbled back to take my bow. She bowed and then walked away, her hair still pulled back in a neat ponytail.

My sensei was laughing, but stopped once I hobbled over to him, putting a stern look back on his face.

"How you like special competitor?"

I bowed deeply to him—and met his eyes on the way up so he could see I was done with my arrogance. I understood the lesson he had taught me.

I limped all the way back home, which was my father's additional form of punishment. He refused to pay for a cab, mumbling, "Didn't I teach you anything, Volodya? Don't ever buckle under pressure. That's the Russian way, that's being a man."

To explain to him that this was my first advanced match was a waste of time. I cursed myself for inviting my parents, since I hadn't invited them before, instead waiting for them to see me in advanced competition. He would remind me of this humiliation for years to come.

My mother had a pained expression on her face the whole way home. She held my elbow. I was glad for the support, though it didn't help. Once we arrived home she had sympathy, letting me lie on the bed while a cool cloth soothed my head.

Compared to the humiliation of being publicly beaten by a little girl, the physical injuries came secondary. I hoped that my classmates would not find out about what happened. I had made an infinite amount of progress in one year, finally getting the bullies to stop beating me and then this happened. My head throbbed, the pain of this memory for years to come.

In bed, rolling around in misery, I longed for the wisdom of my sensei. I longed for the respect, the fear he instilled in his inferiors. When the referee asked him a question between matches, I saw that even he stepped back when my sensei approached. Understanding how to get this power was the key. Once I knew how, it would take me to another level. It would propel me up and out of public housing. Away from this miserable life.

Putin nods at the mobile. Gosha presses STOP.

"That's enough for tonight."

Gosha swipes his phone off the table and throws on his coat, foregoing his scarf and gloves until he's outside. The longer he stays inside, the more tasks Putin can find for him. It's midnight and he'll be home in five minutes. Only an hour lost.

"Goodnight, Gospodin Putin."

No response as usual.

He runs to his apartment building, up the stairs and opens the door. He shrugs off his coat and tosses the scarf and gloves on the hardwood floor. The studio encompasses forty-six square meters (500 square feet). When Gosha first came to Moscow, he started working immediately, so he hadn't time to decorate or buy new furniture and rugs at Ikea. On his first day off, he ran out to a local furniture store and overpaid for a microfiber tan couch, television stand, bed, dresser with a mirror and a kitchen table with two chairs. Then he picked up a TV from the electronic store around the block and lugged it back to the apartment. He spent a small fortune to have all the furniture delivered the same day because he knew he wouldn't have a day off for a long time after that.

All of the furniture in place, Gosha had scanned his hovel, happy with the outcome, ignoring the chipped paint on the walls and beat up hardwood floors, which could use a good refinishing. He was proud of himself. Twenty years old and he had his own place right off Red Square. At least the Kremlin paid his rent.

Blin!

He'd forgotten to buy rugs. His bare feet would be cold in the morning, since he scurried to the bathroom and back to his room to dress.

Oh well.

That would be another venture for another day off. He went over to the back of the TV and squatted to find the cable wires. After hooking them up, he grabbed a beer from the fridge and sat on his couch and clicked on the TV.

That was a good night, nearly twelve years ago, Gosha reminisces as he tears off his tie, collared shirt and suit pants. He changes into faded jeans pulled up to his waist and snug around his bottom. A tee shirt flies over his head, down his arms and onto his body. He's ready for a beer and mindless television. He grabs a pillow from his bed and lobs it to one end of the sofa.

He lies down, putting his beer bottle on the hardwood floor. As it turned out in twelve years, he never did find enough time to buy those rugs and a coffee table. Gosha settles in for a night of watching reruns of *Star Factory* and dozing off on the couch.

Inauguration Day

It's May and the memoirs continue, Putin revealing bits and pieces of his life to Gosha in the depths of his office. Sometimes he sounds like a hero, sometimes like a victim, but mostly, he sounds like himself, the old Putin, the one who Yeltsin selected as prime minister in 1999.

Today Putin almost smiles as his wife and daughters stand beside him. He even puts his arm around Lyuda, a light embrace, to which she nearly flinches, but remembers the cameras in front of her. Her mouth swings upwards like a watermelon slice. Photographers snap away, as Lyuda screams inside at more years as a president's wife, but then she feels the mink stole draped across her shoulders and the cream Hermes bag hanging from her fingers. She smiles.

In a small room in the Kremlin, Putin sits down with a reporter from *TIME* magazine.

"President Putin, you've been in power for twelve years. Was this your master plan all along?"

The translator switches his words to Russian. Putin embellishes a long pause, and the reporter, Gosha and secret service hold their breaths. Then he begins to speak. It is a rehearsed response. Everyone loses interest except the reporter, who has to listen.

However, later that night, Putin surprises Gosha by giving him the real response, in the limo, returning from his inaugural party.

National politics were not a goal of mine.

In 1991 after the collapse of the Soviet Union, state jobs were eliminated. Private sectors opened up, overrun by the oligarchs, the wealthy group of Russian Jews who gobbled up the state's resources like demonic Pac-men. They bought everything in private auctions for dishonorably low prices: oil, mines, telecommunications...My options were to work for these henchmen or work as deputy mayor under Anatoly Sobchak, the mayor of Piter. I chose the most appealing option.

I liked working for Sobchak because he was an honest superior. He knew that I still worked for the FSB (formerly the KGB), yet pretended he didn't. It remained an unspoken rule between us. In exchange, I brought in business to Piter by finding prospects from the West. I'd observed Western business practices and how people made their money through capitalist enterprises, and they seemed more logical to me than communism because in capitalism, the harder you worked, the more you received.

So I worked hard for Sobchak and more money followed until I was able to build a dacha right outside of Piter. Upon its completion, I stood there and stared, smelling the freshly cut wood. I opened the door and peered inside: two bedrooms, a bathroom, a playroom for the girls and a sauna.

Then one day, due to faulty construction in the sauna, the house burned to the ground along with all the money we had saved. We didn't put our money in banks back then. Our life savings were stuffed in drawers, hidden under floorboards. Standing outside of my dacha, watching it burn to embers, I could swear I smelled the money burning too. I told this to Lyuda, who in turn rubbed my back. Tears fell down Masha and Katya's faces as their Western luxuries such as Barbie dolls and makeup kits dissolved into smoke and ashes. This moment changed me because I realized everything could be destroyed at a moment's notice. I had to find security for myself and for my family. I had to become a career man.

That same week the state charged Sobchak with corruption and he fled the country. Our offices had been raided and seized for evidence for the court case. My FSB superior called, assuring me I wouldn't be indicted in this mess. He'd get me out of Piter as soon as possible.

When I was called to Moscow, I didn't consider myself a politician, but I did see the power in the position. Cars, expense accounts, personal assistants. Especially while other Russians still lived in communal apartments. So I committed myself to politics in the 1990s, starting at the bottom and working my way to the top until I caught the eye of Boris Nikolayevich Yeltsin.

He was a charming, intelligent man who could not battle his addiction to alcohol. It consumed him completely. He fell down on stages, slurred his words during speeches and embarrassed Russia at every opportunity he received. Part of me felt sorry for him, part of me was disgusted by his ridiculous antics. We covered up many Yeltsin mishaps, stepping in and handling the President's business. I often took the reins when this happened, using my KGB skills to divert attention the other way. For example, if there was a negative article about him in the newspaper, I'd hire a producer to put together the best clips of Yeltsin and air it on television for seven days straight. As much as we diverted the bad press, the Russian people grew more and more impatient with their leader. I observed Yeltsin's demise and noted what the people wanted: the opposite of him. They yearned for a leader who was young, innovative and sober.

I wasn't high up enough to go, but I received word about the height of the Yeltsin problem, which escalated on a trip to Washington D.C. American President Bill Clinton and Boris Nikolayevich had dinner where, of course, Yeltsin got drunk, yet managed to control himself throughout all three courses. When he went off to bed the advisors on the trip breathed a sigh of relief. Then, in the middle of the night, they received a frantic call from the White House. Security found Boris Nikolayevich running around on the second floor in his underwear yelling, "Pizza, pizza!" They escorted him back to bed and locked his door from the outside. Fortunately, the White House didn't leak any of this to the press, yet we knew they laughed at us behind our backs.

When I became Yeltsin's fifth prime minister, my cabinet and I kept Boris Nikolayevich out of the public eye in an attempt to clean him up. It proved useless as he ordered more alcohol, drinking at his desk or passing out on the couch in his office. We couldn't keep alcohol from being delivered to him. Who was to deny the President's direct orders?

Finally the Duma deemed him unfit to lead. Surprisingly, he agreed. A few months later, in December 1999, he turned to me and said, "You, Vladimir Vladimirovich, will succeed me as acting president."

I was shocked.

"Me?"

"Yes, you Vladimir Vladimirovich."

Boris Nikolayevich was having one of his good days. He was sober enough and alert; his offer to me wasn't a slurred rant or a suggestion before passing out. He meant it.

I felt like I was ten years old again, in front of my physical education teacher. "Why?"

"Because Vovka, you are ready."

On New Year's Eve 1999, he stepped down and handed the country to me. As we left the ceremony, Yeltsin grabbed me by the shoulders and looked at me with earnest. He said something I'd never forget.

"Take care of Russia."

Victory Day

It's husband-finding day, as Gosha had promised himself months ago. Tanya now asks for the rent every month, instead of finding a new job with better pay, or what Gosha hoped for, a new husband. The money is a smaller portion of his salary than he gave to Mama for all her hospital bills, rent and other expenses, but it prevents him from achieving his goal of amassing thousands to become rich.

Tanya's looks are plain, like his, but she has startling green eyes that would make a person call her pretty. Her body resembles a potato-picker, short and dumpy, big bottom and large thighs and ankles. Meanwhile, Gosha stands tall, pale and anorexic thin. He needs to choose a suitable candidate within her league. The single, rich men he knows, oligarchs or sons of former KGB or FSB men Putin favors, would go for models, actresses or socialites. Yet he couldn't choose an average worker because he wouldn't contribute much to the household. The potential husband should take care of Tanya.

Gosha scrolls through the address book on his mobile. Sergey. No, he's a drunk. Misha? No, he's a gambler. But what about Arkady? He's ugly but of even temperament and comes from a nice family. He works as head of the maintenance staff at GUM department store, and his salary is twice that of his sister's. Gosha dials his number.

"Arkady, my old friend! It's Gosha Golubev."

"Gosha, how good to hear from you."

"Listen, are you busy tonight? I'd like for you to meet my sister."

"Doesn't she live in Piter?"

"Her company sent her here for a few days to look over their books."

"Ah. A date, you mean?"

"Yes."

"What does she look like?"

As if pockmark-faced Arkady has the right to ask.

"She's pretty. Very nice green eyes."

"How's her body?"

Gosha lifts the mobile away from his ear and stares at the phone. "What?"

"Her body. How is it?"

"Uh, well, Arkday, that's an awkward question for a brother to answer. See for yourself tonight."

"Okay Gosha, I trust you."

Before hanging up, they agree on a time and place. He calls Tanya.

"A date?"

"Yes, with my friend Arkady. The one from GUM. I met him when I lost my keys at GUM and he found them, do you remember? Then I went out with him and his friends several times?"

"I thought you didn't like him that much."

"Oh no, Arkady is a nice guy."

"Doesn't he have pockmarks all over his face?"

"Yeah."

She sighs. "Fine."

Gosha relays the time and place they'll meet to which she says, "I'll look for the guy who's ugly as death."

"Keep an open mind."

Wednesday night serves as the weekly dinner in public for Putin and his wife. However, Gosha can sneak out for fifteen minutes before the dinner to make sure Tanya shows up for the date.

He runs across Red Square, his light coat flapping in the mild breeze. He enters the western-facing café at GUM. The smell of strong coffee and a beef-onion *blini*, crepe, floats up Gosha's nostrils. He looks around, over the people standing in line to find Tanya and Arkady sitting in a quiet corner. She leans into the conversation yet her chair butts up against the French window. Arkady beams. He gazes into her green eyes like a hypnotized patient. Gosha notices a slight movement of his friend's shoulder every so often. A tic and pockmarks.

Tanya stands up, so Gosha backs away. He silently thanks her for wearing dark jeans and black boots, which slim her chunky bottom half. Arkady watches her ass as she moves, enjoying the packed cellulite. It forms the shape of an upside down heart due to the miracle of good denim. Satisfied, Gosha leaves the café and rushes back across the Square to go to dinner with the Putins.

The next day, Tanya phones Gosha.

"He's okay."

"Just okay?"

"He's already in love with me."

Gosha laughs. "You're confident."

"You want me to get serious, Gosha, to marry him? That's your intention?"

He stops laughing. "I want you to be happy. I want you to be taken care of."

"I want the same for you."

They have nothing to say for a few minutes. Gosha listens to his sister's soft breathing.

She says, "We're kind of sad, huh?"

"Yeah, we are."

He smiles, sure that his sister is smiling on the other end too.

"Gosha!"

He turns around to see Putin walking down the hall.

"I have to go," he says and presses the END button.

"Yes, Gospodin Putin."

"The memoirs. We're not done."

"Yes."

They retreat to the study once more; this time Putin opens the patio doors and goes to the black iron dinette. He pulls out a chair, which scrapes against the stone patio, and sits. Gosha does the same. Up in the sky, the moon lights the area with its genial rays. Gosha unbuttons his suit jacket to get more comfortable.

"Gospodin Putin, we've covered your childhood and many of your political experiences."

"Yes."

"I gave the dictated notes to your publisher. They think you need something else. 'Something more emotional, more revealing,' as they said."

In the moonlight, Putin's face changes from stoic to thoughtful.

"As in?"

"They want a memory, a story that'll pull in the reader. Give them a look inside the 'real' Vladimir Putin. They want you to let down your guard and tell of a memory, a story that haunts you. They asked me to ask you a specific question."

He turns to Gosha. "Which is?"

"'Out of all the experiences you had as president and prime minister, which event affected you most?'"

As he hits PLAY on his phone's recorder, Gosha already knows the answer.

Narva

August 12, 2000 Saturday morning

I pick at my breakfast of black bread and cold cuts. With the tine of my fork, I lift a lone, blond hair from a glob of mayonnaise. A stringy, greasy lock. I drop the fork on the plate, turning my concentration to a cup of tea. Quivering steam rises. I look down at the china cup as it begins to shake as if controlled by an invisible, Parkinson's-diseased hand. The shaking stops. I look around to see nothing is disturbed then grab the handle, wondering if I just had a hallucination. I shrug and go back to drinking my tea.

Today is a day I've been anticipating as president of Russia. Our navy is to conduct a submarine exercise in the Barents Sea. The *Kursk* has to be ready for spying games against the Americans in the Mediterranean this autumn. We've already hunted them down, causing a panic in their navy. Our spies had documented this. We can overtake the Americans beneath the water, terrify them into submission—a feat not even achieved in the days of the Soviet Union.

The *Kursk* is an Oscar II class submarine, which means it is a cruise-missile sub designed to attack NATO aircraft; it's fitted with the highest technology and wrapped in a double hull. My experts assure me it can withstand a conventional torpedo attack. It's a pet project of mine. I joined the committee six years ago, overseeing plans and allocating funds for the construction. It's been a long six years, waiting for every detail to be aligned correctly.

The *Kursk*'s length equals two jumbo jets. It's five stories high and sixty feet in width. Ten airtight compartments guarantee the safety of the 118 sailors aboard. There are twin nuclear reactors and twin propellers. The launch tubes hold twenty-four giant cruise missiles, which when fitted with nuclear warheads, can wipe out entire cities.

Gosha knocks on the door of my hotel suite and slips into the claustrophobic space between the frame and door. He closes it quietly and stands right in front of me.

"Gospodin Putin, I have a message for you."

"From whom?"

"Defense Minister Sergeyev."

"Speak."

"The *Kursk* is loaded and the battle exercise is about to commence. Everything is going as planned."

By late morning, I haven't received any updates about the submarine exercise. But I'm not worried. I've been working with Igor Dmitrievich Sergeyev since my days as prime minister under Yeltsin. I know Sergeyev's system: no news is good news. He hesitates to bother me on vacation. And rightfully so.

Where the hell is Sergeyev? The defense minster is not answering any of Gosha's calls. Nor are any of his inferiors calling Gosha with updates. He always receives a call. Sometimes it's a confirmation call. Sometimes it's Sergeyev telling him to fuck off and let the navy do its job. But he hasn't heard a thing from him or his sniveling inferiors, and that gives Gosha a gut-wrenching feeling. He doesn't want to deliver bad news to his boss. Not now, not on his vacation, not when Putin is about to celebrate his hundredth day in office. Whoever delivers bad news to the boss is the fall guy in Russian politics. Gosha has only been in the game for a couple months, but he found that out quickly. He can't be the messenger. The messenger gets shot.

I decided to travel to Narva, Estonia for my first vacation as president. I always visit the same places, my dachas in Sochi or outside of Piter, or the one in the Greek islands. Instead, I chose Narva to delve into my father's past on the anniversary of his death. My mother died shortly before him, but if she were alive, she would've reminded me of how Papa preferred his years in the military undisturbed. With both my parents dead, I am ready to take this journey.

We leave the hotel. My security, Gosha and I walk on a paved path toward the Narva Castle. Gosha has arranged a tour so I can learn the history, the World War II history. I look across the Narva River, back to Russia, to the hillside town of Ivangorod. The dachas, painted in deep reds, resemble the Scandinavian farmhouses I had seen in that film as a child.

As if someone had dropped a monolithic boulder, the ground suddenly rumbles. Ivangorod shakes, but only for a second. I look to my left and my right. Then everything is still again. It wasn't a hallucination this time. I felt the ground vibrate through my shoes.

My security speaks into their microphones.

"Gospodin Putin, we must take you to this building first."

We change direction and climb a small hill of sparse grass.

Gosha follows them, left behind in the hurry. No one cares about his safety. His heart beats faster. The footsteps of security's heavy shoes pound on the ground, crushing innocent patches of green grass. In the Narva River, concentric circles ripple, as if a beast lies beneath the water.

Once at the top of the hill, I enter a modern building which is nearly finished with its construction. Solid and firm.

"Gospodin Putin, please stand in the doorway."

I stand and peer down to the medieval castle where my tour awaits.

The next thing I know, the ground awakes from its slumber. A wave undulates under my foot, the floor ebbing and flowing. I grab onto the sides of the doorframe. The air pressure swirls, running dizzying laps around my head.

The medieval stones from the castle loosen between the cement. I stare at one in particular as best I can, the scene quivering in front of me. The stone jostles in its resting place, the hole gaping wider until it can no longer remain in place...falling, falling.

Windows break in chiming discord. The castle tower folds into a cloud of grey smoke and it snows white paint chips. The blue sky shakes with fury from the trembling below. Lenin topples to the ground then lies on his side saluting in the grey-and-white-coated grass.

Without warning and without a noise, the shaking stops. The atmosphere is an inhalation of breath waiting for the next tremor. But it never comes.

Rubble is strewn everywhere, on the grass, on the small sandy beach, already floating in the Narva River to Ivangorod. I can't see the town through the dust of ashes and embers. My eyes water from the particles blowing in my direction, and I cough from the stone and cement settling in the back of my throat. The smell of burnt wood and other building materials collide.

The people who reside in the red dachas won't be able to fathom what had just occurred. In this part of the world, these things don't happen. There are no fault lines or shifts in the tectonic plates. No volcanoes nearby. I grew up less than two hours away by car in St. Petersburg, and in my lifetime, there were never any earthquakes.

My security guides me farther into the building, away from the destruction and polluted air. I look back to see a man crawling out of the rubble.

Maelstrom

He tries to catch his breath. Dust rushes into Gosha's mouth, making the task impossible. His cough is dry and husky. When the earthquake struck, he cowered behind security and flattened himself against a wall. He didn't know what to do in an earthquake. He grew up in St. Petersburg. There are no earthquakes in Piter.

His boss stands in a doorway—apparently the safest place during one of these things—surrounded by secret service. They protect Putin like the golden man he is. The President's blue eyes permeate through the thick layer of dust on his face.

Security swamps him with handkerchiefs and water, but he ignores all the pampering and walks outside, into the maelstrom.

I remove my tie and use it as a makeshift rag, holding it to my mouth to filter out the smoke. My eyes water and embers torment my lashes. I have the urge to claw out both of my eyes, but instead I walk down the hill. My security forms a shield, trying to deflect oncoming smoke. I keep my head down and amble slowly, staring at the ground through the slits of my eyes. It's impossible to see anything, yet five minutes ago, I saw a man crawl out of the rubble.

I kick over wood and stones and listen for guttural pleas of help or unmitigated groans of agony.

My head of security says, "We don't see him, Gospodin Putin."

I stop, my feet swathed in charred wood and pieces of stone. The heat from the epicenter grows unbearable, so I remove my suit jacket, unbutton my sleeves and roll them up. I smell the dying embers.

During a substantial break in the smoke, I look into the horizon. Ivangorod, from what I can see, seems virtually unscathed. Rocks fell off the cliff face and roofs are damaged, but I don't see the same full-scale destruction. Through the shroud of grey smoke, Russians emerge from their dachas, putting their hands to their foreheads, searching to understand the obliteration.

I stare back. They don't know it's me. The distance between us is too great. I can't see the panic-stricken faces.

Emergency teams have yet to respond. Perhaps Narva hasn't an emergency team, or all the buildings are destroyed. I listen for the sound of nonexistent ambulance horns and police sirens. In their place, my security and I scuffle atop the fragments and kick aside small rocks.

Gosha follows behind his boss, watching everywhere he steps. How does Putin see where he's going? Gosha can barely see a thing as he trips over debris while hacking up gloppy sludge that rises from his lungs. He stumbles until he trips over his own two feet and falls on the ground—luckily, not falling on any shards of glass. He reaches into the soft lining of his pocket and feels around for his phone. It's intact. In case Sergeyev calls him.

I stop and turn around to see Gosha on the ground, covered in dust like a piglet.

"Go back to the hotel. Get a flashlight."

Bumbling and fumbling Gosha, a young man who is not unintelligent, yet lacks confidence and knowhow. Normally, I'm amused when his antics put another leader on edge, especially one I don't like, and there are many of those. But today, he's not funny.

My security calls out into the destruction, hoping for an answer, but an echo responds. In the distance, I hear the wail of a small siren, the unmistakable sound of an ambulance on its way. I shout to my security to halt the search to let the rescue workers take over.

About to start my walk to the outside rim of rubble, I kick aside a charred piece of wood. It splits. I lift my other foot to take a step, but it doesn't move. Something has latched onto my ankle.

Who I am

He's a large man, around two meters tall. As Gosha asks the front desk for a flashlight, an emergency team rushes in with him. The President is in the midst of the chaos, listening to an emergency worker tell him that the town is using the first floor of the hotel as a hospital. The actual one has been damaged beyond repair. So far the old man has been the only one brought in.

Blood drips onto his salt and pepper beard, spilling from a deep cut that slices the space between his eyebrows and runs down to his nose. On his feet are heavy boots laced up with thick strings. A military-style Russian hat lined with fur sits at the base of his head, and a traditional Estonian wool sweater covers his upper body.

Winter clothes? In the blazing August heat?

The emergency workers push open a hotel room door then transfer him carefully from the stretcher to the bed. The man lets out a cry of misery. Putin stands behind the workers, arms crossed, staring down, his face a mask of ash and dust. He's hardly recognizable except for his pack of hovering secret service. The rescue team takes the man's blood pressure, pulse and checks his facial injuries. The President, Gosha and secret service leave the room for the man to be thoroughly examined.

Putin stands out in the hall. Gosha checks his watch. It's afternoon.

"Gosha."

"Yes, Gospodin Putin."

"Have you heard from Sergeyev about the *Kursk* exercise?"

"No, Vladimir Vladimirovich, I haven't. Would you like me to phone him now?"

"He will call."

Sergeyev is used to the Yeltsin way of command. In other words, Yeltsin answered to the oligarchs or his own daughter, Tatiana. But I answer to no one. Yeltsin dismantled the power structure, and I intend to fix it, to get rid of the waste on his old staff. I wouldn't allow the oligarchs to control anything. They have their businesses, but they won't be attending Duma meetings or instructing me on how to run the country, and in the near future, they will be handing their businesses over to the state. No citizen should own all the oil production, mines or telecommunications in the country. That's the state's job. In a meeting last month, I told them who's in charge.

Boris Berezovsky baited me with the Star of David openly displayed in his matted chest hair. I held my composure, but it made me sick. Roman Abramovich, a frightened pup about to piss on his chair, nodded in agreement. He called me a few days later to assure me that he was on my side. The other oligarchs sat in stunned silence. Except for one. Out of the corner of my eye, Mikhail Khodorkovsky glared.

He is the oligarch to watch, a very intelligent and youthful man, but a threat to the state if he consumes resources at his current pace. He's amassed a fortune in his oil company, ignoring the needs of Mother Russia, unwilling to share the profits. He sat quietly in that meeting, but too quiet as if something else was running through his head. Trendy glasses hid his eyes, so I couldn't read them, which frustrated me because that was what I'd been trained to do with distrustful people.

I'm convinced Khodorkovsky thinks he's above everyone, having this overly self-assured air about him. He makes comments behind my back, very nasty things he has no basis in saying, but the most dangerous thing about Khodorkovsky is that he loves to write. My sources inform me that he writes baseless propaganda about how Russia should be, in other words, his view of a better Russia, where all of the oligarchs would take over. His only intelligent decision is not distributing it to the people.

I will not lose power to anyone, especially the oligarchs and Khodorkovsky. After this vacation, I plan to return to Moscow and clean house. I've come too far to go back to where I started.

The Old Man

Back in the hotel hallway, one of the emergency workers opens the door and closes it behind him.

"Gospodin Putin, is this man a relative of yours?"

So they recognize me despite all the dirt and dust on my face.

"No."

"Is he traveling with you?"

"I don't know him."

"Oh. Gospodin Putin, this man is very injured. He's an older man, probably in his seventies, he suffered a deep laceration from his brow bone into his nose. He'll need a large quantity of stitches. In addition, he has a severely bruised back, two broken ribs and a broken ankle. He's lucky he's not paralyzed or dead. We hooked him up to an IV."

"Is there internal bleeding?"

"Not that we can tell, Gospodin Putin. But the doctor will be here shortly to examine him. The machines that survived the earthquake are being transported from the hospital over to here. We'll know more answers by tomorrow morning at the latest."

"You don't know the man?"

"No, but our emergency team came over from another town once we heard the news. Narva is a place where everyone knows everyone else, especially within the Russian community. I'm sure the doctor or one of the nurses will recognize him."

The emergency workers leave the man's room in a line. The head worker, who spoke to Putin, nods and walks away. The President opens the door and walks inside the man's room. He takes a hotel chair, carries it over toward the bed and sets it down. Worry, concern, fear...Putin's stare does not evoke any of these emotions. In fact, he looks emotionless.

The man reminds me of my father.

The anniversary of his death is tomorrow. When I saw the man crawl through the rubble and then when he disappeared, I thought of Papa, old and helpless. He wasn't such a tall and burly man as this stranger; he was small and compact, like me. I insisted to my team there was someone in the rubble, and when he grabbed onto my ankle, I felt a sense of relief. There was a human being.   Despite his weakened state, the man gripped my ankle with the force of a young man and didn't let go. I bent down and began to remove the debris enshrouding his body, yelling to my security to help. By that time, the emergency workers had arrived at the scene, stopping their vehicles with a hard shove on the screeching brakes. I dug out most of his head, able to see the side of his face. A darting eye. Then someone tapped my shoulder.

"We will finish."

I must have looked unrecognizable because the emergency workers didn't address me in an official tone or with an official greeting.

They removed the rest of the rubble, stabilized the man's body and loaded him onto the stretcher. A groan escaped from his mouth.

Silently, I sit at the man's bedside—a reminder of Papa's deathbed.

In and out of consciousness, my father struggled, his heart waving the white flag of surrender. I had him moved from a hospital in Piter to the best military hospital in Moscow. Once he arrived, I had him placed in a room with a large picture window with a view of the park outside. He could barely talk and wasn't breathing on his own. But when we arrived at his new room, roses and tulips blooming outside, he turned to me and said, "Close those goddamn curtains."

I acquiesced. The curtains remained closed for the rest of his time in the hospital.

After work I would rush over and spend the evenings. We didn't talk unless he asked for something or responded "yes" or "no" to my few questions. I would sit there in the dark with the curtains drawn and watch his shallow breaths, his chest barely moving. The machines beeped and slid up and down.

My phone had rung one night. I wasn't allowed to answer it in the hospital due to its interference with the medical equipment, so I jogged down the corridor, inhaling the antibacterial scent of everything around me. Pushing open the exit door, I answered the phone.

The voice on the other end said, "Vladimir Vladimirovich, you are the new Prime Minister of Russia. Congratulations."

One of Boris Nikolayevich's trusted advisors called me.

I said "okay" and snapped the phone shut.

As Yeltsin's fifth prime minister, I wasn't certain I would last very long. I'd been hearing rumors from colleagues that Yeltsin's advisors mentioned appointing me, but I didn't believe in hearsay. None of them actually approached me and said: "We're considering you." Instead, Yeltsin and his staff preferred to keep privileged information to themselves. The phone call surprised me, but at the same time it didn't.

I swung open the exit door and hurried back down the corridor to return to my father's side. That night was the worst of all the nights so far. His eyes closed as he sputtered out breaths. He coughed up phlegm and choked on it. I'd asked the nurse earlier if there was anything they could do and she said, "No, your father is coming to the end."

I pulled up a chair and sat beside him.

His eyelids opened.

"I'm Prime Minister."

He looked at my nose then at my forehead and opened his mouth to speak, but nothing came out except the rotting smell of his breath. The respirator breathed in and out, a *bayan* rising and falling. The nurse entered and peered over him.

"I'm sorry, Vladimir Vladimirovich. He doesn't have much time left. It's best to say goodbye now."

He hacked an empty cough. Despite his limp from battle, in his healthy years, he had a broad build, thick neck, strong arms. Bulging eyes. But on his deathbed he was a waif. The eyes that were his trademark sunk into the back of his head.

He cleared his throat with the little energy he had left and said, "My son is like a czar."

He sputtered out more coughs for a while then his head fell to one side. The machine stopped pumping, the occasional beep turned into a flat alarm.

The nurse rushed in.

"We must take him to the morgue."

I peered down at him, a mere heap on the bed, the limp body resembling a prisoner of the gulag. I reached out to touch his arm one last time.

My mobile rang. I glanced at the number; I had to take the call from the Kremlin. So I left the hospital to go outside and talk with an advisor about my morning duties. Several minutes later, when I returned to the room, my father's body was gone. The curtains were open to the setting Moscow sun. The sheets had been stripped off the bed and the smell of antibacterial soap filled my nose.

As a Believer of the Orthodox faith, I knew my father's soul departed to heaven. To me, heaven was not a place in the sky, but was God itself.

I turned around and left the hospital for the last time.

At the Kremlin my colleagues effused congratulatory praise. Staffers pandered to my every need, even more so than before. No more typical government lunches. I had sushi brought in from outside restaurants. I replaced my standard government-issued car with a black Audi, with a custom-ordered 007 license plate. If only my father had been there to see how I'd finally made it.

During this time, I didn't tell anyone that Vladimir Spiridonovich had died until several days later. I met with Yeltsin in his office.

"Boris Nikolayevich, I will need to arrange a burial for my father. He died recently."

He motioned with his hand for me to come closer. I did. He stood up, dropped his hand on my head and rubbed it. Through his vodka-soaked mouth, he slurred, "Poor Vladimir Vladimirovich," as he rubbed my head once again.

Typical, inebriated Gospodin Yeltsin.

I stiffened but didn't flinch or pull back.

He stopped and removed his hand from my head, placing it by his side. "You go throw your *batya* in a grave then come back to work."

The injured man from the earthquake begins to stir. He first mumbles then opens his eyes to slits. Wider, they open until he can see I stare back at him.

He jumps.

I washed most of the soot off my face in the bathroom. Though I remain filthy, my face returns to normal except for a few ashen spots I can wash off later in the shower.

He mumbles again.

"Yes, it's me," I say.

The man darts his eyes up to the ceiling, out the window and then back to me.

"Gospodin Putin, what are you doing here?"

"There was an earthquake. You were in the castle when it collapsed. Emergency workers brought you here. You'll live, but you're very injured."

"I was supposed to be your tour guide...where is here?"

"At a hotel. The hospital is destroyed."

His voice scratches like an old record, a moderate whisper, in order to carry on the conversation. The man pushes his body up, the strain in his face showing the pain.

"Don't move. You're very injured."

The man's enormous hand reaches out for a cup of water on the nightstand. It stretches until it encircles the plastic cup. Trembling, he brings it to his lips and drinks.

"Drink slowly."

The man eyes me with suspicion, which morphs into confusion.

"What is your name?"

"Gennady, Gennady Anatolovich."

"You were supposed to be my tour guide, Gennady Anatolovich?"

"Yes."

I check my watch. It's evening.

"We'll speak tomorrow, Gennady Anatolovich. Rest for tonight."

I stand up and walk across the room. As I grasp the door handle, the old man says to me, "It is an honor to meet you, Gospodin Putin."

I leave without saying a word.

Saviors

I awake to a grey morning, the sun edging its way around the clouds. The glare from the sky burns through my pupils like two hot pokers. A night of sleep and my eyes are still irritated and bloodshot from the debris. Outside of the hotel window, at the front of the building, emergency workers roll stretchers and wheelchairs over the cracked pavement. There is no ramp, only stairs. Agile workers reach out with pale arms to lift the victims in their wheeled contraptions. The injured hold their heads or broken arms or legs, but I don't see any major injuries such as with Gennady Anatolovich. No corpses either.

Last night I went to sleep thinking about the old tour guide. He was supposed to provide the answers I hoped to find in Narva. He would know about my father's past if anyone would. He's a Russian living in Narva, and like most Eastern Europeans, probably lived in this city his whole life. Probably fought in the war. Alongside Papa.

I'd found out about my father's past many years ago when I was deputy mayor of Piter. That evening I was in a terrible mood as I rounded the corner on to my parents' street. I had fought through the crowds of high tourist season on Nevsky Prospekt. I unbuttoned my spring jacket and opened it up as sweat poured down my temples and a slight onion smell wafted from my armpits. Breaking free of the chaos, I elbowed my way through the crowds and finally was on my parents' street where I ran into a mass of blond-haired people speaking a colorless language. I'd heard it many times before. Estonian. They hoarded the sidewalk, spreading out like cockroaches all over the cement, and in their large group, not one had the courtesy to step aside for a pedestrian to pass by.

Immersed in the rhetoric of their tour guide, a gangly man who held up a large blue flag to lead his sheep, the people refused to move though my approaching footsteps got louder. I pushed right through the middle, shoving against the dough-like flesh of old women. They responded with nasty insults in perfect Russian, cutting remarks which had no accent. Murmuring continued as I walked up the stairs of my parents' apartment building and opened the door.

Cabbage and liver were already on the table as I let myself in. My father sat at the head, with a snifter of cognac he must have started on well before I arrived. I said hello to both of them to which my mother greeted me from the kitchen and my father nodded, not to interrupt the documentary he was watching. There was Lenin, in an unrecognizable disguise, on the screen. His face clean shaven and his wig of white faux hair morphed him into the Finnish man he was pretending to be. My father had seen this program several times as I remembered the narrator's script almost word for word. This fascination with Lenin, I had no idea where it stemmed from—maybe that my grandfather was a cook for both Lenin and Stalin, but that was a guess. Stepping inside my father's head was an impossible task.

During dinner we cut through tough meat with serrated knives, scraping the plates, which I'd bought for my mother as a gift several Christmases ago. She relished the set of dishes and I knew it pained her with every scratch we added, but it was the only way to slice through the food without being impolite and informing her of her inadequate culinary skills.

We dined in silence, the sound of the knives making up for the lack of conversation until I remembered the Estonians.

"There was a tour group of Estonians hoarding the sidewalk right in front of your building when I walked in—"

"More meat, Volodya?"

"No. Anyway, those people are rude heath—"

My father's hand slapped the table so hard the drinks shook, including his cognac which spilled onto the placemat.

"We do not speak badly of Estonians in this household."

A reaction like this was so out of character. I sat there, unable to respond. The expressionless, emotionally devoid human being I'd known all my life had left his body. Who was this person?

"OK…why?"

"They saved my life once, Vovka, that's why."

"Saved your life?"

"Yes."

"How?"

"During the war, in Narva, that's how. This discussion is over. Mariya Putina, more cognac."

The discussion was over that night and for the rest of his life. I'd never filled in the missing pieces, even my mother wouldn't talk about it. I was dubious she knew more than I did and questioning my father was not an option. He would've thrown me out in the middle of dinner if I kept pressing him, or he would've stopped speaking to me for a great length of time, subsequently upsetting my mother.

He knew how to make those around him suffer. I was well aware of this innate ability. I'd been a victim of it many times.

The phone bleats, interrupting my daydream. I pick up to hear Gosha announce, "Gospodin Putin, I will connect you to Defense Minister Sergeyev."

As I wait, I think of Igor Dmitrievich Sergeyev, the defense minister for the past three years upon Boris Nikolayevich's appointment. He has a bald head, wears tan sunglasses at all times and never smiles. He smokes more than anyone I know, dashing out a cigarette in one hand while reaching for a new one with the other. Most important, Sergeyev was the head of the Strategic Rocket Forces, in charge of securing and transferring nuclear weapons from the Soviet Union to Russia. Missiles are his expertise.

The line clicks.

Sergeyev breathes like an obese American.

Then in a scratchy, smoke-filled voice, he says, "Good morning, Gospodin Putin."

"Igor Dmitrievich, tell me about the submarine exercise."

"Vladimir Vladimirovich, the news is not good."

It isn't his actual words, but the way he says them. His voice sounds distant, almost mournful. I tighten my grasp around the phone cord.

"Yes."

"The *Kursk* has exploded."

I drop the phone cord. It thumps against the wooden desk. The shuffling of my security outside the door, the emergency vehicles driving up and down the street, all of these sounds fade away. Adrenaline surges throughout my cells, shooting to my muscles, one in particular, my heart. It pounds.

"Gospodin Putin, are you there?"

Rapid heartbeats abuse the inside of my eardrums, as if I have a migraine.

"Vladimir Vladimirovich, are you—"

"Yes."

I lift what feels like wooden legs and walk over to the desk chair. I sit down and stare out the window. Sergeyev rushes through a rehearsed speech.

"The submarine has sunk to the bottom of the Barents Sea, just off the northwestern part of the Kola Peninsula. Unfortunately, we don't have radio contact with the crew. We're in a dismal situation because the *Peter the Great*, the sub monitoring the *Kursk*'s exercises, does not have the equipment necessary—"

"And the condition of the nuclear reactors?"

"We don't know."

"And the sailors?"

"We don't know."

I watch another victim roll out of an ambulance. He seems fine.

"Our diving bell hasn't been tested in years, and as you may know Vladimir Vladimirovich, the Russian navy doesn't have any deep sea divers."

"How did this happen?"

He sighs. "We don't know, Gospodin Putin."

For over six years I sat in meeting room after meeting room, choked by the smell of dirty ashtrays. Smoke rings violated my face as I heard about the indestructible *Kursk*.

"Indestructible."

"Invincible."

"Gospodin Putin, it can definitely withstand torpedo attacks."

Not once had anyone discussed the scenario of problems from within the hull. The submarine exploding. All I kept hearing was the *Kursk* had an escape pod, a device that could lift 115 men to safety from the depths of the ocean. For those three remaining men, commanding officers, they would simply wait for the escape pod to be sent back down to rescue them.

How fucking naïve.

We conceived a clean, full-proof plan, but the escape pod, our savior, probably blew up as well.

"Are they dead?"

"We don't know the condition of the escape pod, but our sonar has picked up tapping, possible sounds of SOS signals knocking against the hull. Therefore, we believe some of the sailors are still alive."

"How does the navy plan on rescuing them?"

"We're prepping the *Mikhail Rudnitsky* as we speak, Vladimir Vladimirovich. It's our only rescue vessel. We plan to submerge later this afternoon."

He pauses. I say, "fine" and hang up.

The adrenaline surges, my face and insides heat. I put my hand on my forehead and rub. All I can think is how much time? How much time do the sailors have left before the oxygen runs out? Days...hours...minutes?

Meanwhile...Down in the Kursk

Who will save us?

Lieutenant Captain Dmitry Kolesnikov asks himself this question. In the closet-sized compartment the sailors curl up on the floor or prop themselves up against a wall. The light flickers on and off. For hours the shock overtook him; he lost the ability to speak or move. He couldn't feel anything. But now, the pain in his head floods every sinus cavity, membrane and fiber of tissue. Despite wearing his emergency escape suit, he shivers, freezing cold from the sea water that rushes into the hull.

He sighs with frustration and anger, unable to construct a plan that will save everyone's lives. All he can do is wait, like the rest of them. In the meantime, he decides he must write. Writing calms Dima, even from a very young age. Though he's not a good writer and hardly educated, scribbling assuages bad habits, such as drinking himself to death as he nearly did a few years ago.

A pen, where's a pen?

And paper, where's paper?

Dima reaches his right hand into his breast pocket and finds both a pen and paper to note the details of his command post duties. He pulls out the tiny notebook with wire spirals, flips it open and begins to write down the names of all the sailors he knows are there, but then he opts for roll call instead, to ensure that he lists the names correctly.

"Roll call! Yell out your names!"

The sailors can't hear him. Either their hearing is permanently damaged from the blasts, or they have the same hearing abilities as Dima: muffled and unable to decipher a single word. When he realizes that no one has heard, he focuses his energy on studying everyone's face, despite the blood, cuts and bruises, to determine who is in hell with him.

There are twenty-three total.

That's how many submariners are left alive on this sinking vessel. He writes the number on his pad and circles it. He then realizes he has yet to feel impact. The sub is still on its descent.

When the *Kursk* exploded, the sound nearly deafened him. He saw bodies thrown like ragdolls, including his own. Tools, ladders and furniture ripped into skin, leaving mangled corpses. Dima's friend, the security warrant officer, died standing, grasping onto the secret codes box. The rushing water and blast destroyed most of the hull. Dima instructed the survivors to follow him to the ninth compartment, where they could seal themselves in, away from the flooding. He detoured to the escape pod. As he crawled into the mutilated passageway, leaning on his right side, feeling his way through the rising seawater, he looked up and found a gnarled, twisted piece of scrap metal. The escape pod. On hands and knees, his body shook from cold and disappointment. He hung his head and wailed from a desolate place, somewhere unknown to him. A while passed until he stopped crying and turned back around to continue on his way to the ninth compartment to join his fellow sailors.

For the past several hours, Dima, the only commanding officer left, and another sailor have been stacking bodies up against the hull by clutching their lifeless hands and feet—the Lt. Captain only able to use his right hand and arm, since the blasts hurled the left side of his body against the steel hull. They throw one ice cold corpse on top of another, Sergey, Rashid, Mikhail. They were his crew, his friends, but he holds his sadness in. He must be the strong one, the officer who was trained in an emergency scenario to instruct the others and keep his crew calm.

Murmansk is at least twelve hours away. Even if the defense ministry orders a rescue mission to save the sailors of the *Kursk*, they have to prepare the diving bells and find deep-sea divers. And Dima knows very well that none of this is available in the Russian navy. The diving bells crusted over with age a long time ago, rotting on the docks of Murmansk. Deep-sea divers are not a part of the navy; there is no money in the budget. In a submarine emergency, the navy is fucked. As they are fucked right now and Dima knows it. But pretending is the best option he has to keep himself and his crew alive. So he rations out chocolate and passes around a bottle of clean water in order to ward off the looming knell.

He sucks on a square of milk chocolate. It tastes sugary and fills his mouth with the one bit of happiness he has left.

It reminds him of his lovely wife, Olga.

Olga is a perfect match for Dima, the big red-headed giant that he is. On a destructive path fueled by Mr. Officer vodka, he nearly drank himself into a coma one night. He did so many times before, yet that one night was almost the end. Teased in school for being an elephantine redhead, the most unattractive of male specimens according to his female classmates, Dima's self-esteem was lacking. He didn't know how to pick up a woman, woo her, seduce her. He didn't even know how to ask a woman on a date. Simply put, the Lt. Captain was too shy.

Until he met his Olechka.

She was the reason why he was "coded" like many Russians before him, to exorcise the evils of alcohol from his body. In the doctor's office he chugged a shot of vodka, becoming very dizzy and incoherent. His heart raced as if it would jump out of his chest onto the examining the table. He had to lie down. Was that a long needle they injected in him after taking the shot? Or was that his imagination running wild? Either way he'd never felt that terrible after drinking vodka. The doctor hovered over him and said, "Dima, you are close to death. The next sip of alcohol you take, you will die instantly."

He never drank again, not even a sip of mulled wine on Christmas.

His Olechka made sure of that. She treated him like a king—always had his dinner ready upon his arrival from sea, laundered his uniform, rubbed his hairy back. She wrote him long letters in his absences and sent them to the address he provided for her. They were poetic. Olga was smart, the opposite of what Dima thought he was, and knew how to express herself through every word. He kept her letters close by, folded neatly and tucked under the pillow in his bunk bed. He read and re-read them until he turned off his flashlight and went to sleep. Because of her, he wanted to express himself better in his letters too, so he read literature. The greats: Tolstoy, Dostoevsky, Pushkin. His finger traced over every letter as he read slowly and carefully not to miss the meaning of a word or the opportunity to use a specific word or phrase when writing to his wife.

A banging interrupts his thoughts. It sounds like a hammer against the steel hull. Most of the sailors slip in and of consciousness so who has the energy to hammer?

Wait.

Maybe it's a diver who has come to rescue the entire crew.

They are knocking to get inside, to break through the hull and save them!

Dima strains to look to his left, excited to follow the sound of the noise.

A young sailor bangs on the hull with an instrument of some sort. A small hammer. The sailor's head leans against the wall as he thumps away like a machine. Dima looks straight ahead, defeated and exhausted, but not to the point where he can sleep.

The Kolesnikovs

August 13, 2000 Afternoon

Seven kilometers from Narva—a safe distance from the earthquake's destruction—Irina and Roman Kolesnikov sunbathe on the beach. In the summertime they come from Piter often, three hours by bus, to relax in the resort town of Narva-Jõesuu. They've been coming here ever since Roman retired from the submarine division of the Russian navy five years ago. Buying a dacha in the Narva vicinity was cheap back then, and convenient, since the beaches were full of Russians and Russian speakers. The Estonians chose to separate themselves, buying up property on the coastline farther south in Parnu and Haapsalu.

Roman spent more than a month trying to convince his wife to buy property in Estonia. She opposed the idea, since she didn't understand why they had to travel so far. Most Russians living in Piter preferred to buy a dacha right outside the city, but her husband had these grand ideas. Hadn't he had enough of sea life?

Roman had constructed a convincing argument. If they bought a cottage in Narva-Jõesuu, their sons, Dmitry and Aleksandr, would have a place to bring their future grandchildren. After all, Dima is a newlywed, it's only a matter of time until he and his wife Olga have children. Once Dima returns from his submarine mission, his parents assume that would be the next step.

Olga was a surprise to them. Dima proposed after a month of knowing her, and though it seemed fast, it came as a relief. She was a good influence on their son, cutting off the wild ways of his youth. Their other son, affectionately known as Sasha, Dima's younger brother, was not necessarily wild, but he was mischievous and at times a troublemaker. Roman hoped that following in the submariner tradition of the family would alleviate potential discipline problems. They knew it would be a while until Sasha had children as well, but in the end, for Irina and Roman, it was a worthwhile investment.

With the fall of the Soviet Union several years before, the housing market in Narva proved to be extremely lucrative. The dachas they looked at were very reasonable, since the Estonian kroon was low compared to the ruble. However, the homes were in utter disrepair, so most of Roman's first summer would not be bathing in the sea, but hammering, painting and building with his two sons. They bought the dacha anyway—two bedrooms, one bathroom and an outdoor sauna house.

Irina loved her garden in particular because in Piter she only had flower boxes in the windows of their Soviet bloc flat. On her knees at her age, digging through the dirt, she didn't mind all the hard labor as long as her rose bushes, irises and daisies gave the cottage a charming appearance.

After the renovations of the first summer, Irina and Roman began to travel there as often as they could despite her full-time job and his part-time work as a security officer in one of Piter's largest department stores. In the case of a long weekend, they would hop on a bus and go, leaving after work Thursday night and returning home late Sunday. Their sons visit as often as they can, which isn't very often, since they both live in the North, in Vidyayevo.

This time the Kolesnikovs plan to stay for an entire week. They'd asked Olga to join them but she couldn't afford the time off from her job. Irina always extends the invitation to her daughter-in-law because she remembers how lonely she was when Roman went to sea. Now that Dima was promoted to an officer aboard the *Kursk*, there would be many nights of solitude ahead, since the submarine would be traveling all over the world. A baby relieved some of the loneliness for Irina, so she tries to hint to Olga that a little one might comfort her as well. It's hard, being left alone all the time, yet Vidyayevo is a city where everyone watches out for everyone else. And the upside of a husband at sea for eight months of the year is the romance it brings to the marriage. When Roman would return home, after picking him up at the port, Irina would cook a steak dinner and they would dine by candlelight. Afterwards, she'd kick out Dima and Sasha, dress in white lingerie and run around their apartment with Roman and the cat chasing her, until he caught her and pinned her down with silly kisses. When he was away at sea, she would think about this type of reunion or what new lingerie she'd buy or imagine him masturbating on his bunk as he thought about her.

Along the white sand of the Narva-Jõesuu beach, groups of tourists picnic with coolers of food and wicker baskets. Old women in white hats and one piece bathing suits dole out pickles, herring and black bread to other adults and children playing in the sand. Adults discuss the earthquake which demolished the castle area of Narva, glad that here outside of the city, they remain safe. The death toll is zero, but dozens of people are injured, and the hospital still isn't up and running.

Roman dips in the unusually warm Baltic Sea. Irina reads a book on-shore, digging her feet in the hot sand. Her mobile rings as she is about to turn the page of the most gripping part of the chapter. She almost doesn't put her book down on her lap until she glances at the phone and sees it is Sasha. Strange of him to be calling this time of day, thinks Irina since he calls at night after his parents return home from work. Sasha knows they're on holiday though.

"Hi Sanya."

"Mama," he says in a fractured voice that Irina hasn't heard since he was a young boy. Her heart begins to beat faster.

"What's wrong, Sasha?"

"I…well…there's news here. Some bad news, Mama. We don't know if it's a rumor because you know, rumors always start when the sailors are at sea. Most of them end up being false." His voice fades out, choked up by what Irina believes to be tears.

Roman finishes bathing and dries his body off with a towel. He smiles to himself until he catches sight of his wife's face.

"Speak, Aleksandr!"

Others beside them on the beach turn around to see the hysterical woman scream into her mobile.

"The rumor is there were two explosions on the *Kursk* and it has sunk to the bottom of the Barents."

He manages to spit out the words as if that would cut their sting, but Irina feels the pain slash her heart open. She clutches her chest. The brown color on her face she's been collecting all summer long from the sun's rays dissipates into a sickly white.

Roman grabs the phone out of his wife's hand. Sasha relays the information once more. Upon hearing the news, Roman is calm. Rumors swirl in the navy, especially if a superior submarine, such as the *Kursk*, is involved.

"What has our government reported? The defense ministry? Putin?"

"Nothing yet."

"Where did you hear this?"

"One of my trainers heard it from Radio Liberty Russia. Apparently, many others heard it as well because I couldn't walk down the street without being stopped and asked questions. People are taking this rumor seriously, Papa. I think it's true."

"It's not true until the government has confirmed it."

"They're holding a prayer meeting here tonight at the church, for the sailors. The atmosphere of the whole town...everyone...I don't think it's a rumor."

"Where's Olga? Has she heard yet?"

"Yes, she called me. She was afraid to call you. She's trying to remain calm, but I think she's going to lose it soon."

"Go over there. We'll go back to the house and see what we can find out."

Roman sits at the kitchen table, the one he built with his sons many summers ago, and holds a glass of Mr. Officer vodka in his hand. Night creeps through the kitchen windows, yet he chooses not to turn on a light, instead thinking in the dark, pouring more vodka into his glass. He keeps it stored in a special cabinet which remains locked so Dima's demons would not be aroused, pushing the boy to collapse into his previous state. Roman drinks on either festive occasions or during the unhappiest times in his life—when Dima's friends came to Roman, telling him of the horrendous, humiliating things Dima had done to himself; when he and his wife were expecting a little girl but lost her to a miscarriage; when his parents died one right after the other, he drank. It's a tradition.

The entire afternoon, he's been pleading with his wife to calm down and to think positive thoughts. He made phone calls to his former superiors who are still in the navy. Yet when those phone calls remained unanswered, leaving him to stare at the keypad of his mobile, willing the men to call him back, he knew it wasn't just a rumor. The problem was real. Finally, he turned on Radio Liberty Russia, but not before whispering to his wife and giving her a sedative to induce sleep for at least twelve hours. She succumbed to the little green pill, tears wet on her cheeks, her hands balled into tiny fists. As he used to do with Dima and Sasha when they fell asleep on the couch watching TV when they were small, he wraps Irina in a soft blanket and lifts her off the living room couch and transports her to their bed. He shuts the door behind him. Now, with fingers shaking, he clicks on the radio and tunes into Radio Liberty Russia.

It's worse than he thought. They report two explosions that possibly destroyed most of the submarine. Sonar detected tapping on the hull, a possible sign that the some of the sailors are alive. But the reigning theory is they are all dead. A storm approaches the Barents tomorrow morning, hindering any type of rescue effort. He turns the volume down low, nearly knocking over the radio.

Did I teach my son what to do in an emergency such as...? Roman can't remember. The Mr. Officer clouding his brain won't permit him to flip through the files of his mind.

Ration food, chocolate...submarines had chocolate bars for rationing, canned food, water, no FRESH water, oxygen masks, blankets, insular suits, change of clothes...

Lying his head down on the table, he realizes he can't keep guessing because there is a good chance all of these things could've been blown up as well, including his oldest son. Sleep is a priority, since he and Irina agreed to leave on the six o'clock bus the next morning to return to Piter. They would continue on to take the next mode of transportation all the way to Vidyayevo. Hopefully, they would get more answers there with the rest of the families.

As he is about to switch off the radio, the announcer says something about Narva. Thinking it's his imagination, Roman reaches to turn it off and head to bed until he hears the word "Narva" again. On full blast, he hears the reporter through his drunken fog saying that Putin is in Narva somewhere, on vacation to celebrate his hundredth day in office tomorrow. He hasn't left for Moscow yet or even Northern Fleet Headquarters. He remains right here in town. And if this is true, Roman is certain that he's staying at the Hotell Inger, in the presidential suite, where any important official who visits the city would stay.

This presents a good opportunity to talk with the President. He would know more than the radio or his colleagues who left him waiting. In a clouded fog, Roman thinks Irina would be relieved upon waking up that her husband took the initiative and found out the answers to their questions. He's willing to risk being shot by secret service.

Roman shuts off the radio and stumbles over to the front door with the remainder of the vodka bottle in his hand. He throws open the handcrafted door and slams it shut, rattling the leftover glass of vodka on the table.

KGB

The iron footbridge separates modernity from antiquity. I leave the year 2000 and step back into a time period evoked by soundless streets—the absence of old Zhigulis with clamorous mufflers and children playing. The paved streets of Narva revert into the dusty roads of Kreenholm, suitable for a horse and carriage. Abandoned houses line one side of the street, dilapidated and rusting, while on the other side, rows of red brick buildings stretch the expanse of the landscape. As I walk, they hover, a never ending source of housing or factory life or whatever they used to be.

"These buildings remind me of something."

"They look like Auschwitz."

I stop and turn to Gosha, "You are correct."

They're just factory buildings, but my macabre perspective outweighs any rationality, since I haven't received any hopeful news about the *Kursk* as of yet. Sergeyev calls with updates.

"The *Mikhail Rudnitsky* hit the *Kursk*. It was forced to make an emergency ascent. It caught a glimpse of the *Kursk*'s partially destroyed condition. We believe a handful of sailors are alive."

The escape pod had exploded into pieces.

"Compared to the battlefields of Chechnya, 118 sailors is not a remarkable loss."

"Igor Dmitrievich, in Chechnya death is a consequence. With the *Kursk*, it was never an option."

With each conversation, Sergeyev's voice scratches more and loses its authoritative edge, and by the last update, I can practically smell the cigarette ash through the phone.

"A storm will hit the Barents tomorrow. A rescue effort is impossible until it blows over. All we can hope for is a fast-moving front."

"Convene our naval experts once again. Discuss the best option for rescuing the sailors."

I pause.

"How long do the sailors have?"

"We don't know, Gospodin Putin. There have been instances of sailors lasting up to two weeks in the ocean…but with the proper food, water provisions and radio contact. We imagine water must be filling the hull because of the extensive damage. Our best guess? They only have a few more days, probably until the end of the week. After that, it will be a search and rescue operation for the bodies."

Gosha's stomach mews with hunger. His eyes sting from yesterday's debris. Worst of all, he's nauseous, sick from worry about the sailors, his job. When Sergeyev calls with updates, the President has no reaction. He asked Gosha about lunch and requested a cup of mint tea, but that was it. So they roam Kreenholm, Gosha's idea to get his boss out of his hotel room and into thinking mode, clearing his head mode, deciding what the hell to do mode. Yet Putin has not instructed that he return to Moscow or fly to Northern Fleet Headquarters. Instead, he mills around this ghost town as nightfall approaches, while Gosha suppresses his thoughts to keep his position as Putin's aide.

Kreenholm remains untouched by the earthquake except for a few condemned houses, near shacks, that had collapsed. That morning Gosha watched the President as he sat at the desk in his hotel suite. Putin gazed out the picture window at those hurt from the earthquake being carried into the hotel. The victims were situated on the first two floors, many floors beneath. Security deemed it an unsafe situation and proposed to leave. The President said no.

Gosha researched other hotels in the area, but they were much smaller and also in use as hospital wards and temporary residences for displaced citizens. At least, at the Hotell Inger, more than ten floors separate the citizens and the President. Due to security reasons and the mayhem downstairs, Putin had not returned to see Gennady Anatolovich, although he sent Gosha to check on him. The tour guide had been sitting up in bed and sipping on water.

Gosha reads one of the pamphlets.

"Kreenholm Manufacture was established in the nineteenth century. It was the largest industry in the Russian Empire, amassing over 10,000 employees in the early twentieth century. Its textiles received prestigious awards for impeccable quality.

"Water from the rapids kept the manufacturing plant running. The plant was situated on an island. Employee housing, churches and shops were located on the main land of Narva."

"Where's the island?"

"It's back in Russia, Vladimir Vladimirovich. Before the Soviet Union broke apart, Estonians and Russians could pass freely from Narva to the island."

Back in 1975 to advance in any career in the Soviet Union, Moscow was inevitable. I had worked through my adolescence and young adulthood to gain acceptance into the KGB. I'd transformed my studying habits, achieving high marks, instead of the previous sorrowful ones. I became a linguist, absorbing the German language into my bloodstream due to one film: *The Sword and the Shield*. At sixteen years old I watched it over and over, intoxicated by its substance. I wanted to live every young man's dream. To infiltrate Nazi Germany, speak perfect German and live in an exciting city like Berlin while spying on its inhabitants. I couldn't imagine a better life for myself: living in the West, earning good wages, seizing power over anyone at anytime. It wasn't a fairytale; this could be my life. I craved it as I craved the juicy tomato after I saw the film about Scandinavia.

I excelled in my studies and judo tournaments, earning a coveted spot in the law school at Leningrad University in hopes of acceptance into the KGB. As I found out early in my collegiate career, the KGB comes looking for you, not vice-versa. After graduation I waited for almost a year, nearly relinquishing my dream due to frustration. I began to realize I hadn't impressed anyone, and my dreary alternatives were to become a lawyer or join the military. Even though I'd thought a sailor's life would be peaceful as a child, I had classmates and acquaintances go into the military, only to continue suffering from poverty, injury and death. Military service was the only other way to be accepted into the KGB, yet it wasn't for me. Finally, I received the crisp letter and held it in front of me. It smelled of fresh ink, straight from the copier. It said to report to KGB headquarters.

The preliminary agent training in Piter seemed to fly by. Before I knew it, I was standing on the cobblestones of Red Square, looking at the heart of Moscow, the Kremlin. My trainers had recommended me as a full service agent for overseas work, which meant Germany because of my language skills. I hoped for Berlin because it was an exhilarating city at the time, and because I held onto my childhood dream of *The Sword and the Shield.*

At the Andropov Red Banner Institute I trained day and night to achieve my goal of Berlin. Every moment a superior looked over my shoulder. It was a rank system like the armed forces, and I ranked the lowest of the low. They chipped away at me until there was nothing left, then I was built back up into what they wanted—similar to building a computer or a machine. I was a human robot for the state.

I showered at the recommended temperature, took the precise daily vitamins and learned deadly self-defense moves—similar to those in judo—according to the KGB manual. Every time I looked in the mirror, I felt I was a changed man. Emotion became the enemy, so I learned to hide it.

The Soviet Union prevailed. Our girlfriends, wives, children, parents… all came second. The state was our God, throwing religion out the door and heaving it onto the sidewalk in one unapologetic thud. I believed in the nationalist ideology but with some reservations. The practices interested me more.

How to earn the ultimate respect from people.

How to instill fear in them.

How to extract information from them effortlessly, telepathically.

I could control any situation, any person, coaxing them to do exactly as I wanted. I controlled the outcome.

But I had reservations about communism. I had lived in a communist society my entire life and experienced it firsthand. The party's principles were flawed. Simply put, they didn't work if people like Liliya profited from the working class. I attended lectures on this very subject, nodding my head or murmuring "yes" to all the appropriate responses—anything to get one step closer to Berlin.

The most useful part of training was all the methods of collecting information. My favorite was the chameleon effect. The precision to master it was excruciatingly deliberate but if I could do it, it would place me ahead of the others for Berlin. I watched my own movements in the mirror at night, perfecting them in preparation for the final individualized test.

My superiors brought in a sweating dissident.

"Tell me what you have done."

He reeked of body odor, his white tee shirt wet from moisture. His eyes deepened with purple bags and the skin on his face stuck to his bones. Leftover tears stained his cheeks.

He brought his hand to his mouth. I brought my hand to my mouth. He blinked his eyes. I blinked my eyes. He slumped in his chair. I slumped in mine.

"Nothing. I didn't do nothing."

He shifted in his seat once again. I did the same. This dance went on for almost two hours until I finally broke him, my superiors receiving the information necessary to toss him in jail, to teach this man a lesson.

My superiors expected precision in every detail of my work. A strategy had to be planned, detail by detail, not missing any gaps. I learned to calculate what I was going to do and how I was going to do it. When, where, who, why...all of these questions had to be answered before I attempted any plan. If I overlooked a detail, my punishment would be to devise a whole new plan, from top to bottom. My instructor would bang his fist on my desk and scream, "Vladimir Vladimirovich, don't just observe! Every detail must be noted!"

A fly on the wall, I would note the pattern of its wings, the fur on its head, the bulging red eyes. How it anchored its legs to walk and used its feelers for leading the way. The grain of the wood in my desk, I counted the rings and memorized the varying textures. In people I watched their expressions and body language which consisted of fear, disappointment, anger and sadness. Mirroring them was only one technique. With this newfound clarity, I could control them in many ways by unspoken fear. I changed how I presented myself to others, no slouching like before, my back was straight at all times. My eyes did not stray from their target; I focused on who I was talking to by penetrating them with one glance or one long stare. People couldn't look down on me anymore.

Due my judo background, I excelled above my fellow trainees in strength training. In university, I was a judo champion in Piter, and the trainees knew it by observing my skill. If we had to split into pairs during the strength work, they would avoid eye contact with me. Somewhere during university, my body changed from that of a thin man to a compact and muscular one. The skinny arms and legs evolved into defined biceps, triceps and quadriceps. I was small, as my physical education teacher said I'd be, but my body was powerful and intimidating.

I took the first step to gaining more power, which my superiors saw in me as well. Upon being called into the head office, I was finally promoted to full-fledged agent, ready for my assignment, and eagerly awaiting the next words from my superior. On the outside, my face remained still.

"You will be placed in Germany."

I waited for the next words, the words I'd been anticipating since I was sixteen years old.

"Your assignment is Dresden."

On the inside my heart plummeted to the bottom of my chest. On the outside my expression had not changed. I concentrated on not moving a centimeter of my mouth or my face or my hands. They would know if I was upset.

"Thank you, superior."

I hadn't escaped the Soviet Union. I had thought I'd be placed in West Berlin, or at least East Berlin. But Dresden? That depressing, obliterated city I'd read about in textbooks that'd been bombed out in World War II. It was unfathomable to me.

However, an unexpected surprise happened on that fateful plane ride from Moscow to Dresden: I met my future wife, a beautiful airline steward-ess, smiling and amicable. Before I exited the plane, I asked her out on a date to the theater in Dresden. She said she was to fly back to Moscow immedi-ately but on her next trip to Germany, she would be my date.

I hadn't dated many women, as I was a late bloomer. During university, I liked a few girls and went on dates, but there was no one special. To me, like most young men, women posed complications; they were an obstacle when having a career. In the KGB, it was difficult for the agents to have romantic relationships, since we had to keep a large part of our lives a secret.

I was dubious the stewardess would call, and I threw myself into my work. A couple of weeks later she called though and we met on the steps of the Dresden Theater. Lyudmila was a country girl, raised in Kaliningrad. She showed up wearing a light blue dress tied at the waist—in contrast to the city girls who wore sleek black skirts and copious amounts of makeup. Lyuda's blond hair lay innocently straight past her shoulders with small curls at the ends. There was nothing sophisticated about her, yet she was a knockout.

I handed her the tickets as she said, "I haven't been to the theater in quite some time. This is a night out for me." Behind the excitement, sadness crept into her words. I liked it. She was a real Russian, caught in the struggle like the rest of us.

We took our seats in the grand theater at orchestra level where I couldn't stop looking at the gold embellishments on the ceiling. A bad communist at that moment, I wished for a better life. As I glanced over at Lyuda, I saw she did the same, probably thinking the same thing.

We were together ever since, marrying and having two daughters, Masha and Katya.

Our time in Dresden proved more enjoyable than I had expected. We lounged in beer gardens at the end of the work day with our new friends, other families of the KGB. Food shortages were not an issue as in Piter or Moscow. We had plenty of food, causing me to gain quite a bit of weight. Beer sausages, fried veal, potato salad. My daughters attended nursery school and played well with the other children.

Parenthood was strange for me. I had to strike a balance between being a KGB officer, yet showing attention to my girls. I never did find the balance, so I did the best I could, buying them a few gifts here and there and providing a life outside poverty. After Masha was born, when I held her in my arms for the first time, I had an overwhelming sense of protection, as if I was securing a document for my superior. I peered at her tiny face wrapped in a pink blanket and realized that I was the father of a girl. A boy I could handle, but a girl? Then when her sister was born a year later, I held her too, shocked at another little girl. Tea parties and playing dress up were not things I did, but I painted their room pink and watched cartoons with them.

Lyuda handled the girls because I worked such long hours and I was called into work in the middle of the night. She didn't mind though, because she knew what life would've been like if I was a factory worker or something equivalent back in Piter. She relished our life. After a hard day of work, I couldn't speak about it, but Lyuda knew to either leave me alone or talk to me about daily happenings and gossip to lift my mood. Her role as my wife was a mother to our girls, supporter and friend.

We had a house, a small one, but it was a house. I was proud of it, sending photos back to Piter for my parents to see. Most important, we didn't share it with anyone, unlike my parents who still lived with Liliya whose two children were no longer children. Her son served hard time in Siberia for dissident activities and her daughter was a prostitute in Latvia. I hadn't sympathy for them because they turned out to be as vile as their mother. My mother told me as teenagers they often returned to the apartment drunk or high, vomiting on the living room floor. Papa threatened Liliya to move them the hell out or he would use my KGB influence to punish them. The next day they were gone. The old Jewish man died, and I had left, so the apartment numbers dwindled down to five, in other words, a more manageable household. Upon my next promotion I planned to use my connections and have my parents moved into a new, larger apartment for themselves, in the higher end of Piter.

I collected information on dissidents, citizens who spoke out against the Soviet Union. They became more and more vocal each year I lived in Dresden, resulting in more arrests—where they were thrown in KGB jail and interrogated—and breaking up protests. The task became so daunting Moscow sent more agents. As I observed the daily scenes on the streets and in the beer gardens, I had a hard time believing in the system of communism. It wasn't working—anyone could see that, but my superiors in Moscow refused to accept our reports. The Germans wanted freedom, badly, like I'd never seen before and we couldn't keep suppressing this desire. A new energy swirled all around us. A liberalism that couldn't be defined in a textbook. The Germans wanted to be part of the West. They longed for what their relatives had on the other side of the wall.

This energy was palpable, even to us, the enemy. When I stepped out on the streets in 1989, I felt a surge in the people, a new confidence that hadn't existed when I moved to Dresden. In the beer gardens, they talked excitedly about their plans to meet their relatives in the West soon. A few years before, they would've been whispering.

As a superior in the Dresden office, I called to Moscow and told them of this new revolution.

"I don't think we can fight it, superior. It's becoming too large, even for us."

"Then, Agent Putin, we will send more agents to help you."

"With all due respect, you must listen. I'm telling you this isn't just in Dresden. It's throughout the offices of the Soviet Union. We must be prepared for the fall of our nation. We must have a plan."

"There is no plan, Agent Putin, because what you are saying is blasphemous. The Soviet Union will live forever—we are the 'unbreakable union of freeborn republics' as our anthem says. Anyone who thinks otherwise must be a dissident. Isn't that right, Agent Putin?"

"Yes, superior."

I braced for the devastating consequences of when the Union would break apart. I tried to talk with my fellow superiors at the Dresden office, but they wouldn't listen either. A call had been put through from Moscow not to discuss the severance of the USSR. Collecting information, trying our best to break up protests, we were kidding ourselves. I knew it. I knew they knew it, yet we played this game until the very end.

Until the Berlin Wall fell.

Those around me rejoiced. Music blasted through the streets. The Germans danced and cried, hugging each other while spilling beer all over themselves. Once the celebrations ended, I knew there would be consequences for our office. Celebrations often turned into riots, happiness into anger. So we burned and burned all the documents we could in a large oven for days as the festivities carried on. We hunkered down in the building to destroy all of our evidence, and around the clock, we put in calls to Moscow, asking, begging then demanding instructions. But there was no answer.

Moscow was silent.

Kreenholm

The looming columns, white and broad, exfoliate their milk skin in paint chips, revealing a moldy pink underlay. The sun sets behind the Kreenholm building, a structure which belongs in ancient Greece. I squint to read the letters atop. They spell out the words, "Narva Klub." I step back for a better view.

Rotting planks of brown wood board up the windows. Spider vein cracks split the exterior, while impervious coats of thick black decay smear the entryway stone. Out of curiosity, I walk to the entrance and pull the handle of the front door, which proves to be heavier than I think. I slip inside. After wiping my hand on my summer jacket, I scan the room, pitch black as the door shuts behind me. Gosha reopens it. Light fills the space.

Directly in front of me is a mural that spans the entire back wall. A black-haired woman dances as her skirt forms the shape of a balloon filled with air. The man who twirls her laughs with gleaming horse-like teeth. What's so funny to them? Why are they so happy? In my opinion, the artwork clashes. The multitude of colors scratches my corneas. Behind the dancers, there is a fairytale forest of autumn foliage. Children dip their wooden fishing poles in the Narva River as their parents observe from the comfort of a picnic blanket.

My father and I used to fish at my grandparents' dacha. We weren't very good, in fact, most times we hardly caught a thing, but I reveled in the minutes we shared. We didn't speak much on that tiny rowboat my father had built with his father, except for conversations about the weather and fishing conditions. He displayed whatever love he was capable of by baiting my rod first before his, and in the event that I did catch a fish, helping me reel in the line. Once we landed back onshore, the feeling dissipated, and we returned to our father-son routine.

Papa taught me the opposite of how to parent my daughters. I would be accessible to them, a disciplinarian, but they could talk to me about anything. I wanted to be their protector but also their confidante if needed. It helped that my wife provided the adoration and comfort to our girls. Like Lyuda, they would have careers and contribute to society. They'd never be trash like Liliya or her daughter.

What had happened to my father in the war to make him so devoid, so hollow? I blamed myself sometimes because perhaps he was a better man with my two older brothers, both who died before I was born. By the time I came along, I was the curse of the family, a blighted soul who took the place of my brothers before me. Papa had experienced so much disappointment in his life. I knew he had a kind side once, as my mother told me the story of how he nursed her back to health during the Leningrad blockade. Emaciated and unconscious, my mother was pronounced dead and thrown into a grave of decomposing corpses. She awoke in a sea of death, able to call out until someone found her. In the hospital, she recovered slowly, my father by her side, foregoing his rations of food and giving them all to her.

How disappointed he would be in me, not knowing how to save the sailors. He very well knew the deplorable condition of the Russian navy upon his death, since he had contacts in the military. I could hear his voice clearly as if he is standing right next to me; the leftover scent of cognac swirling up into my nostrils, the monotone voice instructing me to find a way to utilize my nonexistent resources. If it was another leader, he would understand and support him, but with me, excuses were not acceptable.

My own father would not support me, but the Russian people would, and that I know for a fact. The least of my worries is their reaction to this crisis. I'd experienced their support firsthand with the Chechen war. Russians understand that death is an unfortunate and inevitable consequence for the good of the state. We all have our own tragedies to compare—from the peasant famines to our family members dying in the gulag to starving for over three years in the Siege of Leningrad. Persecution and death showcases our history. Yet the sailors' families have to be informed and consoled at the right time, not too soon as to cause widespread panic.

I wanted to fly to Northern Fleet Headquarters, but Sergeyev advised me it would be of no use. Instead of concentrating on the rescue, naval officers would pander to their president walking up and down the swaying docks. If

I went to Murmansk, it would be for the purposes of public relations. My trip would not help the sailors, the rescue effort or the navy. I would be in the way. So I decided to return to Moscow tomorrow morning and meet with advisors and naval experts who would present me with a viable solution. Sergeyev's job counts on it.

How would I explain to an entire population, including on the international stage, that our best submarine had exploded? The West, specifically the Americans, would lie to the world and use this crisis to our detriment, twisting facts into heartache and confusion. Tomorrow, a day that was supposed to represent joviality would be marred by tragedy.

Standing there, looking at the social club's interior, I think of what a beauty Narva must've been. A polished marble floor. Now faded yellow, similar to a *babooshka*'s set of aging teeth. In one corner is a small bar, covered with dirt and grime, with plenty of glasses waiting to be filled. Bottles of liquor, clear or amber-colored. Tables and chairs beckon patrons from the new Narva, yet the ghosts of the old city, vestiges of an Estonian past, live on in memory. In the opposite corner sits a rack of clothes adorned with puffed sleeves and crushed velvet, the traditional style used in Shakespearian theater or centerpieces for fashion shows—they went undisturbed for over fifty years, before the war.

You can feel the history in this place: the ancient clock tower chiming five times, signaling the end of the work day at Kreenholm. Workers poured into this club, leaning on the side of the bar, ordering cognac, whiskey, vodka. The bartender concocted a hammer and sickle, a drink of a quarter Vana Tallinn and three quarters Russian champagne. Music blared from the speakers, the men raising their voices in Estonian to hear each other. They talked about "the old days" as most men do, and how the generation behind them denigrated the nation, a common thought amongst any generation.

Cheap liquor kept them warm in the dead of winter. Friendship stifled their fears of impending Soviet or Nazi occupation. They heard news from both the Eastern and Western fronts, from Tallinn and as far as Helsinki that bombs would drop any day. In this little bar, they banded together as brothers during the hardship of war and eventually fought on the front lines in the Estonian Battalion. Over sips of vodka, they accessed the land and plotted maps for bunkers in the middle of the forest where guns would be perched and ready for a Russian or German solider walking into their line of view.

Their wives, daughters and mothers would plant mushrooms in the soil, in the case of a hungry soldier wandering in the copse. These men referred to themselves as "forest brothers."

Then a Russian would walk into the Narva Klub. The conversations would halt. The sea of blue eyes would dart pointedly to his head, invoking feelings of future enemy lines. Instead of turning around and leaving the club, the Russian would march across the marble floor and order his drink, the hardest vodka in the place. The bartender, grudgingly, poured the liquor into a glass and slapped it down on the bar. The Russian swilled the vodka. There was complete silence, not in awe of this remarkable feat, but a concerted group effort to make him as uncomfortable as possible. It worked. He put down the snifter, paid for the drink and walked out of the club, secure in the fact that he would never forge a friendship with these people nor would they ever grow to respect him. On his way home, he thought about moving back to Piter, since his family could have a better life there. He thought about relocating, especially after this reoccurrence and the way the Estonians treated his children at school. He would discuss it with his wife.

The Russian hadn't a chance. The bombs descended upon Narva. The red roofs, cobbled streets and church steeples disappeared overnight. Fighter planes roared over the cityscape, anticipating their next target. Due to the black smoke clouds from the bombs, the women could no longer throw open their windows while baking black bread and mushroom pies. For the first time in Narva's history, doors and windows remained closed. Streets empty. Schools without children.

There were priorities in a war; baking and socializing weren't among them. A historically peaceful nation of people, the Estonians must've been disoriented in the fog of war. Those in Narva fought with heart despite their small numbers, yet in the end, fell to the Soviets, in my opinion, a better choice than succumbing to the Nazis. This social club represents the past of a civilization—inherently separate from the current one in Narva—a civilization that resisted our values and traditions. Ironically, once peacetime was declared, the city was rebuilt into a Russian haven, a place where the Russian man is welcome and where his children can be educated without prejudice.

A tortured scream jolts my mind back into the present. Actually, tortured screams. I look at Gosha, who is looking down the street.

"A drunken teenager," I say.

Gosha nods, turning his attention back to keeping the door open. As I walk up to the mural and put my hand on the laughing man's face, the screams resound, at first in the distance then come closer. I choose to ignore them, rubbing my fingers on the mural's fabric, until I clearly hear my name.

The lights of Kreenholm do not turn on. Windows creak. Heads appear from them, hiding behind sheer curtains. A man walks out of the night, his hands up like a prisoner on the run. Swarmed by secret service, the man does not flinch, instead he calls out.

"Vladimir Vladimirovich, I need to speak with you about my son. My son the sailor. I need to speak with you about the submarine."

My guard begins to escort me into the Narva Klub, but I shake my head. I look at the man, who kneels on the ground, hands behind his head, breathing in and out so hard that his entire body convulses. He is harmless—an overweight, middle-aged man whose voice has deteriorated either from yelling or crying. A single floodlight from a nearby building shines on his woebegone features, the mouth downturned, the eyes cast toward the ground.

As I walk toward him, my secret service aims to shoot. I motion them to lower their guns. The man could be a trickster, wanting to meet the Russian president, or a psychopath. But the unadulterated panic in his voice leads me to believe otherwise. Unless the man is a great actor on the stages of London and beyond, it's not a show. He knows about the *Kursk*.

Even if he's drunk, I have to find out what the man knows before returning home tomorrow. It will determine how well Sergeyev controls his staff, blocking information from the press.

A meter away from the man, I peer down at him, his massive back heaving.

"Get up."

He touches the road with one hand for balance then rises on one leg then the other, standing at full height. He is not as large as the castle tour guide, but he is a tall, heavyset man. His ruddy complexion looks sallow in the blaring floodlight. Beads of sweat spot his forehead and the dark circles under his eyes are similar to an ultimate fighter after a brutal pounding. A stench of cheap vodka radiates from the man's body.

"You wanted to see me. Speak."

He opens his mouth, yet nothing comes out. He clears his throat and raises his eyes toward mine so I receive a good look at the man. He isn't pretending. No one could forge such misery.

"Gospodin Putin," he starts in a quiet yet choked voice. "My name is Roman Kolesnikov. I am a retired submariner since 1995. My son, Lieutenant Captain Dmitry Kolesnikov, is on the *Kursk*."

I put up a hand to stop him. I turn to my secret service.

"Disperse."

They hesitate. One asks if they can perform a pat-down on Roman Kolesnikov. I agree. After thoroughly searching him, they retreat backwards, hovering around the perimeter and calling to the audience to shut their windows and go to bed. A chorus of windows squeaks. The ominous clicks of guns load to fire. I turn to him.

"Continue."

"I want to know any information you have, Gospodin Putin, to give my wife, Irina. You see, she is distraught. I had to give her a sedative to calm her, she's sleeping right now, and has been for a while. Dmitry is our first born and he has a new wife named Olga, and we're expecting to have a grandchild soon. I know you have two daughters, Vladimir Vladimirovich, I know your father was a submariner, Vladimir Spiridonovich, so I thought I could talk to you. I thought you might understand. I want to give information to my wife when she wakes up. I'm sorry for the state I'm in. I'm not usually like this, but I'm upset and, well, I'm not usually such a mess."

"How do you know about the *Kursk*?"

"Radio Liberty Russia."

My entire body stiffens; I have nothing but contempt for the radio station. It dissects my past, reporting I've tortured and murdered dissidents in my KGB days. From the moment I was elected acting president, Radio Liberty Russia has tarnished my image, relentless in its pursuit.

"What did they say?"

"That the *Kursk* has exploded and is in danger at the bottom of the Barents. That most of the sailors have already died. That the Russian government hasn't a plan to rescue them."

No one would've known such extensive details. Except for those in Sergeyev's cabinet. I would confront my defense minister in person. Civilians who engage in government business have the potential of undermining the entire rescue operation. We are Russia, not the West…not America, where public opinion matters more than the decisions of the President. In Russia, the government's word is the final one; no one protests and the few who do are unhinged. The community shuns them.

"What do you think of this whole situation, Roman Kolesnikov?"

"Me?" He points to himself.

"You."

"I—I, I don't know, Vladimir Vladimirovich. I just know that I want my son home safe with his wife and with us. I came here for some informa-tion—"

"To tell your wife. I know. But it seems like you're well-informed. I cannot tell you anymore, Roman Kolesnikov."

"Then it's true? It's really…it's really true."

Sorrow drips from his last three words, the pain of losing a son releases into the air and sits, a gap between him and me. It floats there, an invisible cloud lingering for several seconds then changes shape into a stream of formi-dable vapor, traveling into my body to the dark corners of my mind.

"Go home. Your wife will need you when she wakes up. I cannot help you anymore."

He turns around and walks back in the direction he came. After a short time, the darkness envelopes him. Security dispatches a car and follows him all the way home to ensure that he will not come back.

Sergeyev

Suka, suka suka!

Sergeyev smacks down each notepad on the shellacked table top. As he pushes the secretary out of the meeting room, he says he will distribute the notepads and pens to each seat. He glances at his wristwatch. Fifteen minutes until this fucking meeting. In Putin time that means at least another hour or so, since the control freak of a leader runs everything on his agenda. In the good old days, Sergeyev would drag Yeltsin off his couch and prop him up in the leather seat like a ventriloquist's dummy. He'd have to nudge Boris Niko-layevich when he napped—only if the President had to give an official yes or no. Sergeyev or Yeltsin's prime minister would whisper the correct answer in his ear and let him fall back into dreamland.

A cigarette dangles in Sergeyev's mouth. He lit one in haste before entering the conference room, the secretary staring at him with wide eyes. He keeps forgetting Putin's strict policy of no smoking, which Sergeyev regards as outrageous. This is Russia for Christ's sake, what other enjoyment is there but to smoke? Everyone smokes. His parents, his kids, even the nuns at the monastery down the street—he's caught them lighting up in the courtyard. The next thing Putin would want is prohibition. If that ever happens, he plans to defect to Finland, where they drink all the time. *Can you defect to Finland? Would they want me?*

With fingers yellowed from years of tobacco use, Sergeyev pulls the cigarette from his mouth and looks around for an ashtray. His boss had them removed. *Sykin sin!* Son of a bitch! Sergeyev tries to open cabinets and a few drawers, but they're all locked. Not knowing what to do, he opens his suit jacket and pulls out the suede wallet his wife gave him this past New Year's and stamps out the burning cigarette on it. An ashen hole bores into the deli-cate suede, ruining one of the nicer presents he's ever received from his embit-tered wife. The cigarette sizzles against the soft leather. Sergeyev shrugs then opens a window and throws the cigarette out into the bushes. Then he opens a few more windows, airing out the room, not realizing the Kremlin guard around the corner. Once he sees Sergeyev, he nods and returns to his post.

Advisors pour through the doors, mumbling and clutching their leather briefcases. After the officials take their seats, Sergeyev keeps one eye on the door, waiting for the boy who precedes Putin. Gosha reminds him of a Soviet white mouse in desperate need of a bath. He trips, falls, makes a general ass of himself but Putin likes him, well, at least tolerates him.

Sergeyev reaches for his breast pocket to find a package of cigarettes. His fingers prod and molest the smooth plastic wrapping of the unopened box. The conference room door creaks. He releases his grip, laying his hand atop the table.

Gosha holds the door open for the President then runs ahead of him, pulling out the chair at the head of the table. Putin sits and stares at no one in particular.

"Igor Dmitrievich, speak."

"Gospodin Putin, a stormed raged in the Barents yesterday. It finally blew out this morning, nothing can be done until later. You're returning at the right time because you must make a decision."

Sergeyev waited a full day to tell Putin the *Kursk* had exploded. Once the inferiors relayed the news to him, he thought it was an exaggeration. No need to bother Gospodin Putin on vacation. He would blame Sergeyev. The navy would be vilified. Putin would be vilified. He would fire Sergeyev…or worse.

"What else?"

Putin eyes each member of his inherited cabinet. He hasn't made sweeping changes. Yet.

"Gospodin Putin, Northern Fleet commander Admiral Vyacheslav Popov called this morning from the Barents. He has received offers of international aid, first from the admiral of the Norwegian navy and second from the Brits."

In the hours following the explosions, Sergeyev made phone calls, answered phone calls, summoned advisors to the Kremlin. But he forgot to do the most important thing. He forgot to stop the message.

Admiral Popov had pre-recorded a message of the success of the *Kursk*'s exercise. Sergeyev forgot to call the state television station and instruct them not to run the announcement. It played on television several times, interrupting regular programming. Popov's walrus-like mustache danced along with his words of elation. Sergeyev had watched, in a horrified trance, the smoke from his cigarette blowing up his nose. When he snapped out of it, he contacted the station to halt all airings.

Putin does not speak, so Sergeyev continues.

"As you know, Vladimir Vladimirovich, Popov is an absolute Soviet. He distrusts other nations. He strongly recommends not accepting foreign aid. I agree."

Sergeyev joined the navy many years ago, when the Soviet Union had prevailed. He understood the nuances of the system. The rules were straightforward: do your job and shut up. Ignore everything and accept everything, even if innocent people got killed. Follow orders.

Under Gorbachev, the floorboards of a strict Soviet society had loosened, and by the end of Yeltsin's last term, they had come unhinged. The defense minister had also learned from the oligarchs how to manipulate Boris Nikolayevich to get what he wanted. If he really needed permission for a military problem or crisis, he would talk with the oligarchs and all would be fixed.

"Why do you agree with Popov?"

"We'd be relying on the West, Gospodin Putin. It would make the navy look incompetent. Russia too."

The President says nothing.

Sergeyev hasn't figured him out. The new President has been in office for three months. As Boris Nikolayevich's prime minister, Putin was a "yes man" to the president, mostly silent in meetings and letting the oligarchs run things. When they appointed him, Sergeyev thought to himself, this KGB man may turn on them. He'd seen it many times before in his career—the old KGB did not answer to others. The first few weeks, Putin was exactly what the oligarchs elected: quiet, stoic, but young and healthy. A perfect political puppet. But then power began to shift. Putin stopped listening to the oligarchs then closing off meetings to them. He distanced himself from Yeltsin, but maintained a good public relationship, which included tennis matches and lunches. He changed the rules of the Kremlin, such as no smoking, and much to everyone's demise, no drinking in meetings.

Vodka *was* a staple of the Duma.

"No."

"Excuse me, Vladimir Vladimirovich?"

"No."

"No to accepting aid, a good choice, I will tell Popov. And your decision about the *Kursk*?"

The advisors' heads swing back and forth like spectators at a tennis match.

"Rescue the sailors. Today."

"Yes, Gospodin Putin."

The President pushes back his chair and stands up. He walks the length of the table. Gosha opens the door. Before Putin walks out, he turns to Sergeyev and says, "Today."

Moya Semya (My Family)

August 14, 2000 Monday late morning

The aroma of eggs and sausages lingers.

I enter my house through the kitchen. The staff has finished cleaning up after breakfast and gone on break. The silver sheen of the stainless steel refrigerator greets me instead of my wife or daughters.

The kitchen is reality. Workers have runs in their pantyhose. Boots are made of plastic, not leather. Every day I make an appearance, nodding my approval, walking around the work stations, examining the meats, fruits and vegetables. I inspect underneath their fingernails to ensure cleanliness and glance at their heads, satisfied that hair nets tuck away potential unruly strands.

Two days a week Lyuda and I agreed that Masha and Katya would learn how to cook a meal assisted by the head chef, since living with such indulgences erase any form of a work ethic. Lyuda and I agreed not to spoil our children with material pleasures. I'd made the mistake of spoiling them when they were little, lavishing them with Western dolls and gifts, motivated by my sense of constant lack as a child. After watching my daughters mourn for their lost things in the dacha fire, I reset my priorities. I replaced a few of their toys, and anything else new was a birthday or holiday present.

I won't destroy my daughters' work ethic. Once lost, it can't be recovered. Time would elapse to the day when one of my daughters would self-destruct. Perhaps a marriage to a man who pays her bills. Buys her the finest jewelry. Then beats her each night for no reason at all. In Russia, this is reality, and for my daughters, if I couldn't protect them from this type of future, in the end, I'd only have myself to blame.

Lyuda and I have a system set up where the girls work for extra things. Besides cooking two days a week, they clean their rooms and help their mother with the menial tasks of her fundraising efforts. On my orders, the gardeners disregard fallen leaves. The girls rake them.

Despite being a year apart in age and sharing all of the same experiences, the girls are radically different. Our youngest, Katya, is a lady in all respects, from the pink outfits to the hair clips and braids to cooking with the staff even on the off days. She charms everyone with her ladylike manners and minute voice, and especially her angelic face, which does not resemble mine at all.

Masha, on the other hand, is a ruffian for a young woman. Though pretty like her sister, Masha's mouth contains no filter, a trait that Lyuda and I continue to discipline out of her.

Roaming around my study as a little girl, Masha searched for old books and maps then queried me about the historical relevance of everything she found. She would tear through the entire room and never put anything away.

"Masha, remember the rule. Stay away from the small bookcase underneath the window."

There was nothing of importance in that bookcase, yet she needed some rules. Otherwise, she thought the study was hers. She and Katya used to fight over rooms. One had claim of this room and the other had claim of the other room. And for some reason neither Lyuda nor I had any rooms.

"Yes, Papa. It's your KGB stuff, right?"

"Masha, are you always this fresh? No, it's not my 'KGB stuff' as you call it. I don't have any 'stuff.' Where do you get these ideas?"

"Did you have a gun?"

"Yes, but it was only for protection. As I've told you before I was nothing but a paper pusher."

"Did you ever shoot anyone between the eyes?"

I warned her to stop the nonsense. When Katya chimed in, I reprimanded them both.

Masha possesses a sort of uncanny perception, nothing supernatural or magical, but a heightened sixth sense about others. She can see through a person's façade and eerily dig until she retrieves the truth. If she were an FSB agent, she would be a great interrogator. I like to think she inherited this trait from me, but her talent is innate, where I had to work at mine.

When she was a young child, a government colleague visited our dacha outside of Piter. He spent the day with us, brought presents for Lyuda and the girls. We discussed government affairs and socialized. I liked the man and invited him back. As he got into his car and drove away, I felt a tugging on my pant leg.

"What, Mashenka?"

"Papa, that man is bad. He's not good. You shouldn't have invited him back."

She stuck her lollipop back in her mouth and plodded inside the house. A couple weeks later, I discovered from another colleague that the man had been embezzling government funds and was later indicted. To my knowledge, he still suffers in a hard labor camp in Siberia.

The downside of Masha's gift is it makes her inaccessible to others; she can't sustain a superfluous conversation. Masha sees right through the person. Even me. I'm not at ease with my daughter during the rare times we spend alone. I feel like she reads every one of my thoughts.

Past the kitchen I enter the dining room. The tips of silverware peek out of silk napkins. They adorn the table, which is set for four although there are twelve places. Each setting is spaced sixty centimeters from the other, exactly as I prefer, with Lyuda and I sitting at the heads of the table.

At dinner we let the girls chatter about their day, usually when they take a field trip with their home school tutor, or we dine in silence because I've had an exhausting day at work. From one look at me, my family understands which mood I'm in and acts accordingly. I enjoy hearing about the girls' day because it's a release from my reality and confirms that they receive the childhood I never had. Plenty of friends, parties, luncheons to attend; they certainly do not rely on rodents for companionship. With our status, everyone desires to befriend my girls, which led me to warn them against how people may use them. Masha replied that she had the situation under control. She watches over Katya. I don't have to lecture again.

As I walk into the living room, chlorine fills the air from the indoor swimming pool set in the back. To relieve stress I swim in the mornings and practice judo in my studio at night, inviting my old coach to spar with me on occasion. For a man of forty-eight years, I'm in good health. Sustaining my physical upkeep shows a dedication to my presidency, a definition of what a young, vital, successful president should be. Russians, throughout my duration in office, will have the best of their leader.

The living room resembles a museum with red velvet couches and chairs beautified with gold trim. The banister is made of mahogany wood, which has engravings of the tsars immersed in battle, aiming a gun or stabbing a knife through an enemy's stomach. From ceiling to floor, the windows stretch across the entire front wall, the sunlight warming the otherwise cold room. The house aches as I saunter to my office where I do most of my work when I'm not at the Kremlin. A minute alone there—a familiar place where I make crucial decisions—produces a calming effect.

I walk to the glass doors at the back of my office and open them onto the stone patio. Often, I sit at the iron table, poring over documents, letters and decrees that require my signature. The scene is most pleasant in the autumn with the smell of wet deciduous leaves, and in the sky, the blending colors of the trees with long, black rifles. Snipers perch on the branches and the roof, allowing me to relax, but for Lyuda, their presence unnerves her, especially when she digs for things in the attic and hears their footsteps back and forth.

The image of Roman Kolesnikov creeps into my mind, on the pavement, hands behind his head, trembling, my security poised to shoot the fearful father. I shake my head.

I walk back inside to my desk. Gosha put today's newspaper on it. Besides the standard reporting of the *Kursk*, there is a headline reading, "Putin Celebrates His Hundredth Day." I stare at my photo. The man in the picture stares back at me.

I drop the paper and turn to the small television that I only watch to view the goings on in Chechnya or a documentary about Russian history. In fact, it is covered with a velvet cloth, which I lift and switch on the television beneath. After the meeting with Sergeyev and my advisors, it's confirmed Roman Kolesnikov has heard the truth.

I flip through the television stations to find ORT, owned by my nemesis Boris Berezovsky. They report the norm: the *Kursk* has suffered difficulties and the navy is in the process of a rescue. The reporter announces after the commercial break they'll have a live interview with Berezovsky, who is Russian, but also a Jew. The kind of Jew I hate most.

The Jewish family I had lived with in our communal apartment, they were good Jews, not bothering us. The only noise out of them was the father mending clothes on his sewing machine late into the night. It served as a lullaby; I fell asleep to the hum of those stitches. As a child, I didn't understand why this elderly man with arthritic fingers would constantly work away on his sewing machine, yet I grew to like this old Jewish couple and their daughter. They were kind-hearted, letting me play on their side of the room.

The man had a long beard. He wore a black vest and pants, and a silver pocket watch at all times. I remember once asking how he acquired it, since it appeared quite expensive. "It's handed down from my father," he said. His wife, who treated me like her own child, patted my head and told me to stay out of trouble. The apartment smelled of warm, baked bread on Fridays due to her expertise in cooking. The daughter helped her mother, having nothing else better to do. Not married off to another Jew and in her thirties, her own people forgot her because neither men nor women friends ever visited. As a family, they rested on the entire Sabbath and read the Torah, which lay in a sacred place on a black music stand in the corner of the living room, not to be touched. Even my parents never entered that corner.

The Torah sculpted religion for me. I didn't read Hebrew, but I understood this book was the most valuable thing to these people. A thief could break in during the middle of the night, strip our family and theirs of all our worldly possessions—hardly any—but if the Torah was stolen, that would've been the worst offense of all. Every time I walked by it, I left at least half a meter of space between myself and the book. Milk or food was carried in the other hand, the hand farthest away.

I asked Mama one day, when I was very young, "Why is that book so special?" She answered, "It's their faith, Volodya. They base their whole lives around this book." I didn't understand the book, but I respected it, and so did Mama. As for my communist father, he could have reported this family to the authorities for practicing religion, but chose not to. The family was good to us, especially compared to Liliya. If he turned them in, we'd have ended up with people who were troublemakers, especially if the state were to punish us for harboring religion. And Judaism was the worst religion to harbor. The punishment could have been severe.

Berezovsky is not like the old Jew in my childhood apartment; instead he epitomizes the stereotype of a greedy piglet Jew who happily steals from others, but of course, never from his own kind. He seizes whatever company he wants and bends Russia's laws to do so. A typical Jewish way of conducting business.

He flashes on the television screen, his large head occupying the top half with a cocky sneer.

"I guarantee," he says in that hideous Jew accent, "that nothing is being done to save these men. It is well-known in Russia that the navy is poor and useless. But do you see what Putin is doing? He's treating this like Chernobyl. Following in the footsteps of Russian communism. Once KGB, always KGB."

Berezovsky smirks.

"Remember Chernobyl? Gorbachev stayed silent for eighteen days. This is only the third day. We'll be waiting a long time for an answer."

I switch off the television, my fingers shaking. I get up, shoving my chair so hard, it falls to the floor. I walk across the room to stare out the glass door onto the patio.

I do not have the technology to save the sailors.

I do not have the right to expose our military defense—to endanger every citizen in Russia for 118 sailors. In the Soviet Union, we would've never allowed another country to enter a nuclear submarine, even if it meant saving lives. The sailors would have died quietly, without any media exposure. But this is a different era.

Imagine if we spend millions on rescue personnel and equipment from Norway or the UK. Then we plunge into the Barents and enter the submarine. Only to find out all of the sailors have died in the initial blasts.

So what's more detrimental? Risking the lives of our rescue workers to save sailors who are probably dead…or accepting aid from an adversary country that will exploit our naval secrets? Russia is ruined both ways.

There's a soft knock at my office door, followed by creaking hinges. Masha pokes her head through the slit.

"Papa, you don't look so good. Do you have time to eat lunch with me?"

"No, Mashenka."

"How was your trip to Narva? There was an earthquake?"

"Yes."

"Gosha called to assure us that you weren't hurt."

"That's right."

She opens the door wider and slips her slender frame inside the office. Similar to her mother, her blond hair curls at the ends. She wears a designer skirt and blouse, and heels much too high for a fifteen year old. She looks silly balancing on the cobblestone streets.

"Why aren't you with your tutor?"

"Papa, it's August, school doesn't start until September first."

"Where are your mother and Katya?"

"At a language fundraiser. Mama thought Katya would be best suited because old conservative ladies will be there. Lots of *babooshkas*, lots of fur."

"What are you doing today?"

"Not much. That's why I wanted to see if you had time for lunch."

"Not today, Mashenka."

Protests

In Volgograd, formerly Stalingrad, men and women run through the streets like pirates raiding a city. Banshee screams reverberate. Flashlights wave in all directions. People smash storefront windows. Alarms blare from tipped over cars with government-issued plates.

In Piter, an effigy dangles in the square where Putin grew up. Right off Nevsky Prospekt. It frightens the tourists who turn down the road for an evening stroll. Burning in the moonlight, the stuffed man has a line drawn across his face. Those are his lips, neither in the form of a smile or a frown. Hay springs from the top of his head. Sparse blond hairs. He is stripped naked, a sack stuffed with material to fill out his body. Only a small tattoo—a writing of marker on the makeshift chest where a heart should be—reads the letters: KGB. People stand and stare into the flames. Sweat pours down their bodies.

In the suburbs of Moscow, there is a beautiful villa. Russians elected their president to live here. What is Putin doing now?

The people march on the road to his house, flashlights in hand, against the perched guns of the military, secret service and snipers positioned on the roof. Hundreds of protestors unify their voices into one chant that encapsulates everything.

"DAMN YOU! DO SOMETHING!"

Down in the Kursk

Another sailor gone.

Seven in the past hour.

There are only nine left, barely grasping onto life. The stack of men grows higher. The living spreads out. The compartment turns into a spacious coffin, and it smells of vomit, piss, shit and seawater.

Dima closes his eyes for a long time, not ready to surrender, but just closes them. When they are veiled, it helps, similar to when he was an alcoholic and the world would spin to nauseam. He's never had an intense migraine, though his mother suffers from them all the time. She resorts to lying down for hours in the complete darkness of her room. Sometimes she throws up because they're so intense. Dima follows in his mother's footsteps—he vomited about an hour ago. This is how Mama has felt…all these years?

His family of sailors dies off one by one. They are like no other crew he's experienced. They are brothers. Captain Lyachin makes sure of this. It is he who recommended Dima for this honor, to serve on the *Kursk*, the best submarine in the Russian navy. His position is coveted and many older officers pushed for their sons to receive it; however, Dima's father was retired and didn't believe in nepotism, so he stayed out of the selection process.

Captain Lyachin had noticed Dima on a prior submarine mission, where most of the crew was barely out of gymnasium. Lyachin didn't have time to instruct each officer; he couldn't be everywhere at once. So Dima assumed that role, teaching the young ones. The men were well-trained by him; the Captain had noticed.

"I originally heard mixed reviews about you, Dima," said Lyachin.

"They must stem from my drinking days, Captain."

The times when he showed up late for an exercise, vomiting overboard before they submerged into the water. Reeking of alcohol in front of his fellow sailors. They grew tired of covering for him and talked with Dima's father. He sat his son down for a stern talk, saying, "I hear they're about to throw you out of the navy. I'm so ashamed."

The memory of his father's face burns in Dima's mind, even in his current state. To lose his sea legs forever, that would've been the cruelest punishment of all. He couldn't live without the sea. It gave him purpose, life, a reason for being.

So with a needle and shot of vodka, he got coded in the doctor's office. Sober from his demons, yet drunk with happiness, Dima excelled on the missions and exercises afterwards. He was a leader in the spy games against the *Theodore Roosevelt*, the sub they had hunted down in the Adriatic and frightened off, according to insider spies. His promotion to Lt. Captain made his father so proud that Roman's eyes welled up with tears.

His father was a submariner. Same with Dima and his brother, Sasha, who is not on the *Kursk* because he is new to the navy. Dima has high hopes for Sasha, knowing his little brother will upstage him in every way. He thinks Sasha is smarter, quicker to understand things and stronger in will. But as a precaution, being the older brother he is, Dima receives frequent updates from Sasha's superiors to make sure the boy keeps in line and doesn't fall victim to his elder brother's mistakes. He hasn't thus far.

Dima knows he can't hold out much longer. The oxygen masks are somewhere in this compartment, but he can't remember where he put them. He believes that he distributed them a couple hours ago, but now he can't recall. So he must gather his strength and feel around with his right hand for one. *What day is it?* He feels the icy steel floor then the slick boot of another sailor. He remembers the twelfth of August, when the exercise began. Is it still the twelfth? Maybe it's the same day, maybe it isn't.

He cups a piece of smooth plastic. The oxygen mask. He slumps against the wall and puts it over his face and inhales.

He takes a violent breath, knowing a dead sailor had worn the mask. When Dima was somewhat functional, he handed them out, making sure everyone got one. So many of his brothers are gone—this is the epicenter of Dima's rage.

Why aren't they saving us?

A thought hits him like a Type 65 torpedo.

They think we all died in the explosions.

He rips the mask off his face and plunges into his pocket for the tiny pad and pen. They have to know the truth. He angles the pen to the best of his ability and writes:

We are here, adrift in the sea, actually, maybe we are on the floor of the Barents. We have nowhere to go except to wait here for the rescue. There are twenty-three of us who crawled from the other compartments. We are huddled here in the ninth compartment, some of us dying one at a time, while others die as twins, as triplets. Our missing crew, I presume, have died in the blast, the accident, whatever happened. And now we are trapped, like sardines on a sinking vessel, and you, the military, the people who find us, must know the truth and this is the truth. That you thought we had all perished but we haven't. We honorably serve Mother Russia and we wait for your command. If I am dead by the time you read this, know that I am Lt. Captain Dmitry Kolesnikov.

Dima's head sways from side to side, his consciousness slipping, the grim reaper's fingers coaxing him into the darkness. He welcomes death now. When his body dies, he believes his soul will be transported to God. Once he reaches Final Judgment and passes into heaven, his body and soul will reunite and he will be in nirvana.

He covers his nose and mouth with the mask. It is the reason he has the ability to write the note in chicken scratch, despite the throbbing pain that shoots throughout his entire body. The pain subsides into numbness as he finishes the note, which signals he must be close to passing out. He once read a long time ago that when the human body cannot handle pain, it shuts down. His body does this now. Shuts down.

His heavy eyelids pop open. He can't lose consciousness yet. There is one more note he has to write.

One more person to whom he must say goodbye.

The Kolesnikovs Travel to Vidyayevo

It took Roman and Irina Kolesnikov all day and part of the night to reach Vidyayevo. Roman had a hell of a time changing and riding buses, due to the debilitating pain of a nasty hangover. On the bus, the chatter had not been good for him or Irina. He wished for a car so many times on that trip, he couldn't keep count. Loud mouth people, insensitive to the *Kursk* family members around them, blurted out the worst scenarios for the submarine.

"They're all dead."

"Been dead since the explosions."

"No use for a goddamn rescue mission."

Drunks. Not what Roman had been the night before, wallowing in his heartache over a bottle of vodka. They were mean drunks with missing teeth. From their mouths spewed venomous words laced with the ink-like smell of pure ethanol.

Before riding the first bus, he gave Irina something to calm her. On the second long ride to the arctic city of Murmansk where Sasha would pick them up and drive them fifty kilometers north to Vidyayevo, he gave her another sleeping pill, half a dose so she would wake up in time for arrival. The ride was bumpy in the worn-out seats in which Roman could feel the metal frame. The drunks, used to riding the buses, shoved to the beginning of the line and occupied the shady seats for the entire duration of the trip. The unlucky ones such as Roman and Irina had to sit in the boiling sun, with the smell of body odor and alcohol all around them on a sweltering bus. The windows did not open and air conditioning was nonexistent on buses, the same with heat in the winter. Passengers could draw polyester curtains to shade themselves from the sun, but then they would be forced to stare into a curtain for hours.

The sun scorched. Roman chose to pull the curtain. He reached over his wife to do so, brushing his wrist against her forehead. She did not stir.

To drug his wife was disheartening. He remembered the day Irina and he took Dima home from the hospital, their first born, wrapped in a fleece blanket, an indulgence in those days. Irina insisted her baby's skin touched against softness for the first time. She didn't want the scratchy dishtowels the hospital used for newborn blankets. For Sasha, she used the same one, and if the baby girl had been born, she too would've been enveloped in fleece. Roman knew Irina thought of Dima as her first baby, the way she pampered him when he visited, although he was a huge, red-headed, married baby. That love never diminished for Irina; it remained there after Dima moved away, and left a void in her. When Dima began to visit more often with Olga, the void began to close up and heal. With her son's possible death, it reemerged, but this time would never leave until her death.

On the last leg of the bus ride, Roman wonders about his son. If he is alive, Dima would be consoling the young ones. It's in his nature to do so. If Sasha were in the same situation, he would joke around to establish camaraderie, but his eldest son would use compassion. And Olga, that young beautiful girl is soon to be a widow, a woman who already suffered enough by sending her new husband off to sea and not seeing him for months at a time. Roman sighs.

He anticipates the moment he can climb down the bus steps and see his family to console them. It has been hours on the rickety bus and the drunks had finally drifted off to sleep with dull, gurgling snores. The pain in Roman's head throbs as he remembers the details of last night, such as nearly accosting the President. After barging out of the cottage door in his inebriated state he decided to stumble into town and talk to Vladimir Putin. He was so out of his mind, even the secret service with their guns loaded did not discourage him. In the darkness, through the flood lights, he concentrated on Putin. He was much smaller in person than on television, but his face was the same, stern and unforgiving, unable to answer any questions. In his speeches, he spoke for lengths at a time, and in interviews, he spoke in dense chunks for hours at a time. So Roman was taken aback by Putin's brusqueness, yet at the same time, he was glad that the President commanded secret service not to shoot him. It showed some compassion in Putin; he wasn't a mere product of the KGB.

From the President's tone of voice, Roman believed Putin knew as much as he did, perhaps less, since annoyance crept into his words when he mentioned Radio Liberty Russia. The government hadn't control over the situation, and as usual, the navy hadn't communicated with the Kremlin. For his son, death was imminent.

On his trudge back to the cottage, somehow finding his way back in the black night, he analyzed the duties of his new position: preparing the family for identifying a charred body, if there was a body to identify, and attending memorial services. He'd been assuring his wife all day that until the government pronounced them dead, they weren't dead. To keep hope.

What a mistake.

On the walk back from Kreenholm, he'd thought of how to convert their minds into dealing with the loss of a loved one. His boots dragged along, scuffing the pavement. All he could think of was returning home and collapsing into bed beside his sedated wife.

Irina pretends to be asleep, in order to cope with the endless bus ride of drunken idiots, making rude, classless comments that she'd never say aloud, especially when on a bus full of soon-to-be mourners. Last night was a blur. She knows her husband slipped her some type of pill to relax and fall asleep. The last thing she'd heard before entering into a comatose slumber was the radio in the kitchen and Roman unlocking the door to the secret liquor cabinet. Vodka tumbling into an empty glass. Instead of lying awake hysterical, listening to the radio and Roman's drinking, which indicated her son's death, she chose to let the medicine govern her consciousness. She'd fallen into an ignorant peacefulness, a refusal to admit the truth. She slept until her husband woke her up at five-thirty this morning to catch the bus to Piter. He smelled fresh from a shower, though his eyes were bloodshot and blurry. A whiff of his breath revealed an overzealous regimen of brushing with mint toothpaste. The squint in Roman's eyes signaled to Irina that her husband was extremely hung over. He had packed the night before so all they had to do was call a cab to the bus station. Once she saw the amount of people going on the early bus to Piter, she realized what a long day and night of traveling they had ahead of them. Three hours to Piter, then a fifteen-minute layover, enough time to purchase tickets for a bus to Murmansk, which would occupy the entire day and some of the night. Fortunately, summer consumes the

Murmansk Oblast. In the winter, a dreary grey would add to their depression. Even on August nights, there's an early winter chill in the air.

Irina turns toward the window the entire trip, her shoulder and face nudged against the glass. Her hair shields her face from Roman. She keeps one eye on the furious pink sun. It burns as if a feminine creator set the sky on fire. In the distance, she can see the lights of Murmansk, the northern city dotted with apartment buildings and houses, and in the background, the snow-covered mountain caps.

Sasha picks up his parents on time and drives them in virtual silence back to his home. Irina studies the hardened look on her son's usually amicable face. He hasn't shaved nor cleaned under his armpits. Irina can tell. The black scruff ages him beyond his years and the dilated pupils make him look like a crack addict who never sleeps. He races through the streets as best as he can, but there's traffic. The victims' families have driven up to Vidyayevo for the latest news, support, whatever seems necessary.

"We'll be home in a few minutes. The roads are so crowded…it shouldn't take that long. I know you've had a long ride from Narva. How many hours was that? Oh, I haven't cleaned my place, I apologize, no time. This sprung upon me, I mean upon all of us, but you can have the bed. I bought a new bed last year, actually not a new bed, I bought it off an older couple who was moving back to Moscow and couldn't take the bed with them. Anyway, the bed is huge so you should be comfortable. I bought it in case of guests, but I wasn't anticipating guests this early. I'll sleep on the couch, you can have the bed then. The mattress is a little worn down—"

"It's fine. We'll be fine," Roman says.

"Did—did you have a nice time in Narva at least, well, before…"

"Yes, we did, we were."

"That's good. Good. Good for you."

Sasha accelerates the gas, since traffic moves at a normal pace again.

"Uh, was it warm? Was the water warm, the beach?"

Roman puts a hand on Sasha's shoulder. "We can't pretend things are normal, Aleksandr."

"Yes, Papa."

"Let's be silent the rest of the ride. It'll be easier on all of us."

Taking Off

Gosha stands at the kitchen counter shoveling down a steaming bowl of mincemeat pelmeni. The President swims in the indoor pool. Gosha hopes to be dismissed soon so he can return to his apartment and go to sleep. It's been a long day and he wants to lie in his bed and think about nothing.

As he dives his fork back into the bowl, he thinks about the progression of his mother's illness. Her last doctor visit had cost 6000 rubles for the breast specialist to check her lump before the operation to remove it. He said it was the size of a ping-pong ball. Mama let it grow and grow, ignoring her own bodily needs, either out of fear or financial hardship or both. Gosha pictures his mother cold and frightened, lying completely naked on the metal examining table. The doctor would remove the lump and then make a decision about the breast itself. When Gosha talked with his little sister Tanya, she told him that she heard Mama crying behind the shut bathroom door. She whispered between sobs, "I'm going to lose my breast."

This image makes Gosha weak. What is it like to lose a body part? He cannot imagine. At the time, he understood she would need plenty of rest if she were to have a mastectomy. She would be out of work for up to six months.

More than anything, he wished he had been there for his mother.

He puts down his fork and hears footsteps coming to the kitchen door. He hasn't time to stash his bowl somewhere so he holds onto it, prepared that someone would tell Putin that he's eating his food. He holds his breath.

Secret service thrusts open the kitchen door. Gosha drops the bowl, causing it to break on the tile floor. The guards shove him aside, stepping over the china pieces and smashed food, and stampede the President's house like a herd of wild boars. Gosha ignores the mess and runs after them.

They yank open the door of the pool room. The President is mid-lap. One arm stretches in a perfectly arched position above his head then the other arm. Secret service stands at the edge of the pool. When Putin almost reaches the wall, they shout his name, yet in a respectful voice. About to flip and continue with the next lap, he halts and looks up. Gosha edges closer.

"Gospodin Putin, you must leave now. We have to take you to an undisclosed location."

"Why?"

"There's a mob of people moving upon this house. They will arrive soon. For your protection, we have to relocate you."

"Then stop the mob."

"It's more complicated than that. There are hundreds of people. Not only here, but throughout Russia; we're getting reports of rising protests."

"Protests of what?"

"We're receiving reports there are protests against the government. These people want answers about the *Kursk*."

The pool water ripples.

"We have to move quickly, Vladimir Vladimirovich."

For the second time that day, Gosha packs suitcases. He does so in a mad, but organized rush. His boss won't listen to excuses about wrinkled clothes. He's already packed two leather suitcases, kneeling on the floor of the massive walk-in closet. Putin showers and dresses while secret service paces outside the bedroom. The President acts as if he is about to attend a dinner party, dressing in a suit, putting on one cufflink at a time, combing back his hair, adjusting his tie. Finally when he's ready, he announces, "Let's go."

They walk out of the house to a waiting car. Secret service surrounds the driveway, the lawn, outside the fence that shields Putin's home from the road. As Gosha steps into the car after the President, he hears shouts coming from far away. An entanglement of human voices. He gets in and shuts the door.

The car engine revs and takes off, swathed by the long line of cars in the presidential motorcade. The gates open up ahead and they fly past, turning to the right and speeding along a back road in a northerly direction. Gosha fights the urge to look back at the house, in case it isn't standing when they return. Putin stares straight ahead, never looking back or to the side. Gosha notices a small muscle spasm in the President's left cheek. It pulsates to where he can't control it.

A Complication
August 15, 2000 Tuesday early morning

Masha is in the motorcade.

Apparently, she was in the driveway with her bodyguards and driver—about to go into the city to have dinner with her mother and sister—when secret service stopped them. By the time Gosha and Putin emerged from the house, Masha's car had already been placed in line. She'll ride in another car, but when they reach their destination, it would be her and Putin in a small, tense space. A fight would ensue.

When the Putins fight, Gosha can sometimes escape the room and shut the door behind him. He isn't an eavesdropper because swarms of secret service watch all movement around the President, and because he doesn't want to hear about their problems, especially in light of his own.

The Putins fight in their own unique way. Lyudmila, the matriarch of the household, commands the kitchen, maid staff and her fundraising committee with direct marching orders. Masha and Katya receive them too. Yet with her own husband, she refrains from brusqueness and instead, chooses a tone of inferiority. When she's angry about something, many times the girls behaving badly, or more commonly Masha behaving badly, Lyudmila Putina would talk to her husband in a low voice, as if she were back in the cockpit of a 747 reporting to the pilot. She's that calm, touching Putin on the shoulder and talking to him so closely that her breath hits against his face. Bursting into anger is not an option, even if Lyudmila has the urge to scream and shout, because in the end, her husband wouldn't respond to it. Upon hearing any menacing news, Putin would announce the girls' punishment to which Lyudmila would call it "too harsh for the situation." They would banter back and forth for a minute or so, engaging in a loud whisper. When this begins, Gosha moves to the complete opposite side of the room or leaves and stands outside the door. An argument rarely lasts beyond a few minutes.

Masha nor Katya dare to raise their voices to their father. The girls understand their place in the family although Masha prods her father too much at times. And when she does, Putin has the ability to hide his emotional response.

Only those who spend day in and day out with him could read the President's body language. And only the situations Putin feels most drawn to or that affect him deeply trigger such a reaction. Otherwise, in a room full of advisors, he solidifies into a statue composed of solid rock.

The car ride never seems to end. Gosha glances at me out of the corner of his eye. His knee bounces up and down. We ride in a limo, the freedom of wide space between us. I wish he would open a book or pretend to look through papers, but he continues to look at me out the window, using the reflection of the glass.

Masha is somewhere in the motorcade. My secret service had moved Lyuda and Katya to a remote location; however, I instructed for them to be flown to Berlin. A longtime friend, Gerhard Schröder, the chancellor of Germany, would take care of them. As for Masha, they told me she rides with us, safe and calm, listening to a music player in one of the cars. That last thing I want is for my daughter to be here—this new complication adds to the jumble of other complications.

We reach a small roadside restaurant in the middle of nowhere for a bathroom and fuel break. The restaurant is seasonal, open in the warm months, yet there are no customers on the premises, only the restaurant owner who speaks a low form of Russian and has few teeth. He points me to the bathroom around the back. To my surprise, it's an outhouse, a venture I haven't been on in a long time, since my days of visiting my grandparents' old-fashioned dacha in the sticks outside of Piter. When I was a young boy, I would bring a kerosene lantern when visiting the outhouse at nighttime. I remember being afraid that a large bear paw with sharpened claws would swipe my face and rip off my eyelids, nose and lips. I would be an outcast in society. Yet every night when my grandmother sent me to the outhouse at bedtime, I went.

After using the bathroom, I walk around to the front of the restaurant to see secret service filling cars with their own portable tanks of gas. My daughter looks out to the distance. I walk up to her.

"Do you have to use the toilet, Masha? You should do it now."

"I will, Papa."

"Mariya, look at me."

She turns.

"I did not intend for you or your sister or Mama to be put in this situation. Especially you, right here with me."

"I know, Papa."

"Then why are you so quiet?"

"I'm thinking about the sailors."

I take a step back.

"You've heard?"

"Yes, Papa. It's all over Radio Liberty Russia and ORT and a couple other places. I wish you would've told me, but I guess you couldn't. I knew something was wrong when you came back from your vacation a few days early and without notice. Mama wasn't expecting you either."

"Don't be scared, Mashenka. Mama and Katya will be fine. You and I will be fine."

"What will happen to the sailors?"

"It's complicated."

"There's 118 of them, right?"

"Yes."

"And they have wives, children, mothers and fathers?"

"Of course."

"They've been down there nearly three whole days now."

"Mariya, stop. Go use the bathroom. We'll be on our way again shortly."

"Yes, Papa."

Masha walks out of sight around the building. I look down at my watch to discover that we've been traveling for hours, much longer than I had originally thought. I know we're driving to somewhere along the Russian border. I call out to security to ask how much longer the ride would be to which an officer replies three more hours. We'd be pulling into our destination with the rising sun.

On the road once more, Masha rides in my limo. The smooth pavement of the well-traversed roadways transform into the potholed back roads of the Russian countryside. Every so often we pass a lone horse, cow or fenced-in vegetable garden on a farm. In the fields, dachas stand with their graying wood and arched roofs, and behind each of them is a copse.

The provinces.

Every time I drive through the villages, I'm reminded of the real Russia, so far removed from the flourishing city centers of Moscow and Piter. If you're an average Russian, this is how you live, and often with a broken-down car instead of public transportation. This depressing country life equates to communal living in Piter, and shockingly, even in the year 2000, it exists. A report came across my desk recently documenting over 300,000 families still live in the *kommunalki* in Piter. Why don't they move out to the country? They'd have a better life, property of their own. But there's silence in the country, nothing but your own thoughts to fill the time. I understand that people need the daily grind of city life for pleasure and purpose. And to escape the boredom, the invisible force weighing down the sagging power lines.

"Papa, do you miss Dyed?"

Gosha turns his body toward the window and taps away on his phone.

Masha's grandfather, her Dyed, loved his two granddaughters very much, and in particular, he and Masha had formed a special bond. Katya and her grandmother, her Baba, were more attached, spending hours on end baking treats, playing tea party, dressing up. Not Masha. She favored Dyed, and in turn he favored her. They had an unbreakable bond I could never understand, since I barely heard my father utter a word throughout my childhood and adolescence, but somehow Masha and he had long conversations. They understood one another.

They would take long car rides together around a year or so before my father died. The rides turned into a tradition upon each visit to my parents' dacha outside of Piter. I had no idea why. My father told me Masha enjoyed seeing the countryside so he'd take her fishing up at the lake, yet I never saw any fishing poles. When I questioned him, he replied they made their own. Then I asked where the fish were and Masha said they released them back into the water upon a catch. They synchronized their answers, countering my hesitation with an exact response. One thing was for certain, I was being duped. But I let it go because Masha seemed happy and safe, and I wanted her to have a relationship with Papa—the one I never had.

"You must be sad. Dyed died a year ago. And you've been, well, you've been—"

"I've been what?"

"You look so worn down, Papa. I've never seen you like this."

"You know I have a lot to think about, Mashenka. Being president is a twenty-four hour a day job, I can't switch it off. We discussed this before I became president."

"I know, but—"

"Mariya, listen. You should not interfere in my political business. You are too young to understand any of this."

"Papa, I am in your political business. It's a round-the-clock job for me as well, being the president's daughter. It never ends."

"You're lucky, Mariya Putina. Look around you. Look at this country-side. This is what you could've been. A young girl out here would change places with you in an instant. You should not act spoiled; your mother and I did not raise you that way."

Gosha becomes more absorbed in whatever nonsense he's doing. He's grown used to the spats, since he's overheard them many times. When I first became president, my daughters were wary of him; now they speak as if he's not there.

"Don't you miss him, Papa? Do you remember the first Christmas in our new apartment when we moved to Moscow?"

On that Christmas, I showed off my new apartment to my parents. I'd been working long hours in the Moscow government to achieve the dream of a spacious, luxurious apartment for my family. We had three bedrooms, each deep and long, unheard of in Moscow. Lyuda painted the walls a rich off-white color and moved in furniture, not old and ratty from a secondhand store, but brand new furniture wrapped in plastic. After Lyuda unwrapped the dishes and glasses, I would snatch the bubble wrap out of her hands and pop each bubble. We had one bathroom, yet it was a clean bathroom, inside our apartment. I couldn't hear another person except my own family day and night, due to the cement floors. The apartment was a motivating step to owning a house again one day, as we did in Dresden where we enjoyed dinner in our own backyard every night, cooking in a barbeque pit.

There was a knock on the door. Usually I waited for Lyuda to answer it, but that day I wanted to see my parents' faces. I marched a straight path to the door, Lyuda and the girls in tow, and swung it open. There were my parents, fresh out of a car service from the airport where they flew in from

Piter. My mother clapped her hands together and said, "Volodya, look at how far you've come! This building is so fancy!" She referred to the ornate balustrades in the stairway, the vaulted ceilings and dangling chandeliers. Then she peered past us into the apartment and gasped. My father looked too and shrugged his shoulders. My face heated. Once I had entered politics in Piter many years before, my standard of living had increased and I had sacrificed so that my parents' standard of living increased along with mine.

My anger subsided as my daughters rushed past Lyuda and me, pushing us away with their tiny hands and running to their grandparents for hugs. My mother enveloped Katya in a long embrace while my father picked up the already tall Masha and, despite his bad leg, swung her around as she giggled with delight. She possessed a magical power that made my father human.

"I missed you, Dyed!"

He hugged her even harder, and scratched her cheek with the scruff of his beard. She squealed. He placed her on the floor next to her sister. She took his hand and skipped as they headed toward the couch.

"Do you want to see the apartment, Papa?"

"No."

"There's the grumpy, old man I know," I mumbled under my breath.

"What did you say, Volodya?" asked my father, his eyes narrowing.

"He said, 'there's the gru—'"

"Mariya Putina, enough!"

"Yes, Papa."

Masha raced to the kitchen and dragged a step stool across our new tile floor. A cupboard opened and glasses chimed.

"Mashenka, what are you doing in there?"

"Leave the girl alone, Vova," my father said.

I glared at him.

"Umm, I'm trying to find a cognac snifter for Dyed. Papa, where did you put the bottle of cognac?"

"Mariya Putina! Get down from there! This isn't the behavior of a young lady. You should know better. Leave the stool there; don't drag it across our new tile floor."

"But Dyed—"

My anger about to spill over and ruin the day, my father looked at me and said, "Mashenka, it's nothing. Just come sit by me and we'll watch some TV. Your father can find me the cognac."

He patted the place next to him on the couch as she ran back into the living room and plopped down against him.

About to yell at her for leaving the cupboard door wide open, I caught a glimpse of Katya in her bedroom with Lyuda and my mother. She showed them her doll collection, which was spread out over her pink comforter. Then I looked back to Masha and her grandfather who had settled in to watch a documentary about Nazi Germany. I sighed. Why can't Masha be more like her sister? How did I conceive this strange child?

As Lyuda and my mother prepared dinner and Katya helped by setting the table, Masha and my father continued to watch the documentary in silence. I joined them, watching the liberation of a concentration camp by the Russians and the Americans. Even for me, it was a horrid sight in black and white, the ghostly bodies of naked men, the shaved heads, the hollow eyes. The skin was so tight around their faces if it stretched anymore, the flesh would pull apart. I was about to turn it off for Masha's sake, when she turned away from the screen and looked at me.

"Can I have the *petushok* that Dyed brought?"

"Not before dinner."

"Oh. Okay."

She turned back around and continued to watch the program, forgetting all about the lollipop.

Dinner commenced at our polyurethane dining room table. My mother ran her hand across the smooth surface and commented, "How beautiful." I smiled, glad of her presence, giving me the reaction I craved.

"Your apartment, Volodya, is magnificent," she continued, "I can't believe how far you've come from communal living."

"You should've seen our house in Dresden," Lyuda added.

I eyed her. She changed her wistful tone. "But it was nothing compared to this. I much prefer it here."

Lyuda stared into her plate and began to cut her meat. We all followed suit, silver clanging against the china. During the meal, Masha insisted on throwing a spoonful of the traditional Christmas *kutya* on the ceiling for good luck. I sighed and granted her permission, since I didn't want to assume the role of spoiling the fun. The kutya stuck then later during the meal fell down in one big plop on my father's head. She and her sister couldn't stop giggling. My father smiled, removing the lump of porridge with a napkin. He sprung up from his chair and ran around the table, dragging his bad leg, trying to chase my daughters in every direction. He caught them both in each arm and picked them off the floor. He tickled them until their eyes flooded with tears from laughter.

I didn't know how much more I could take. Uncomfortable, I shot a pained look to Lyuda, who seemed to be amused by the whole thing. She caught my eye and reached across the table, putting her hand over mine, and winked. That small gesture calmed me down as my father set the girls back on the floor and we resumed our dinner.

"Yes, Masha, I remember that Christmas very well."

"So do I, Papa."

I glance at my watch.

Two hours to go.

Hiding

My motorcade splits. Most of it drives off in the distance. Four cars, including mine, turn down a dusty country road that resembles a potter's clay—a taupe, dried-out earth embedded with small rocks and fissures. I've been awake the entire night. The rose-colored sun creeps through the overhanging trees. My body is on a high of no sleep, over-awake, over-stimulated, my eyes darting at the scene around me.

Masha has fallen asleep beside me a long time ago. Gosha remains awake though I saw him flutter his eyelids a few times then look at me.

As the car slows, leaves and thin branches grate its steel panels.

Birds chirp outside the window.

The car comes to a stop and doors open. Then mine. I step into the pleasant morning breeze and follow secret service on a short walk on what appears to be a cliff face or small mountain. Brush pushes against my face and clothes. I look behind me to see that Masha sleepily follows.

Agents part tree branches, revealing a rusty fence running along the cliff's edge. One pulls out clippers and cuts a hole. Close in the distance, on the other side of a stagnant waterway filled with sludge, jagged rocks and clumps of aquatic plant life, I see a similar fence but with an electrical shock system and warning signs in Russian to keep away. Below in the valley, overgrown trees strangle buildings with decaying facades. It's an island.

It has to be Kreenholm island. I'm back to where I started three days before.

I follow secret service and descend a steep set of iron stairs etched into the fading rock of the cliff. Shaking, the steps seem like they would break away at any second and I'd fall into the soundless brook below. Our footsteps clang on the stairs and secret service splashes into the shallow water. I wait on the last step until an agent nods in a direction and I follow, selecting the flattest and driest stones. I expect a hidden or movable bridge or platform to be laid out for me, yet they hadn't enough time to prepare, or the path to the hideout is kept like this to deter outsiders. Either way, it's a perfect ruse; both Russians and the West would never think to look on a decrepit island.

We weave our way through a maze of factory architecture. Buildings cracked and split, the roots of plants bursting through the seams. They grow into long vines and wrap the buildings in their octopus-like grip. Because of exposure to the elements, metal doorknobs and decorative trim have rusted to an orange-scarlet color. Roofs on several structures have collapsed from water damage. A large pack of termites gnaw a hole into a rotting piece of wood plank. My feet stick to the ground as I trudge along. It's a swamp. It certainly smells like one. I'm in an untamed jungle.

Hidden by leaves and brush, secret service has to move the plant life aside for the opening—a factory door made of fresh pine. The silver knob shines. I wonder if Yeltsin knows about this place; had he been taken here?

I enter the factory room, absent of machines. An apartment replaces it with couches, a television to monitor the news, a table and chairs and a small kitchenette with a stove and oven. The room has rugs and pillows and a radio sitting on a large desk shoved in the corner.

"Gospodin Putin, there is a bedroom in the back. And a bathroom. We will set up here in the living room and start working," says an agent.

There are no windows or other doors. Camouflaged guards stand with large guns outside the hideout. My stomach turns. An image of Gorbachev pops into my head, the coup in 1991, Yeltsin standing on the tank.

In judo practice and tournaments and in the KGB, I was sharp and alert, aware of everything and everyone around me. Luxuries had accompanied the premiership then the presidency, making me lazy. I hadn't chosen a new cabinet upon taking office. I follow secret service, like a blind man following his walking stick. I should've called my KGB friends and gone over each detail.

I could be suffocating under my own paranoia, but my instincts lead me to believe that I'm being lured out of the presidency, quietly and without a fight. And like the submarine, I'm naïve enough not to have a backup plan.

I watch secret service set up a station on the desk and living room table. Papers crinkle as they unfold. Television switches onto the news. They tap watch faces and check mobile phones. This appears to be a well-rehearsed play. And I'm the lone audience member.

I have to find a way out.

"Masha, go to the bedroom. Get some sleep."

"Papa, are you okay—"

"Go."

She scampers across the floor and shuts the door behind her.

Secret service surrounds the hideout, the entire island. There's one door leading to the outside. I scan the room for any escape routes. I slip in the bathroom then enter the bedroom, closing the door as not to awake my sleeping daughter.

"Papa?"

"Mashenka, why aren't you asleep?"

"I can't sleep. I'm not wide awake, but I'm not tired either. Where are we?"

"Next to Narva."

"This place wasn't destroyed in the earthquake?"

"Apparently not."

"Do you think Mama and Katya are safe?"

"Yes."

"Do you think we're as safe as them?"

I turn to my daughter. "What do you mean?"

"Never mind, Papa."

She rolls over and turns her back toward me, yanking the covers over her blond head.

Hours later and still awake, my head aches. Brown spots float in my vision from watching too much television. I stand outside the factory. Hidden under the canopy of trees, I can't get what I saw out of my head.

Snipers shooting from the roof of my house, the crowd uncontained, screaming and crying out obscenities. Secret service grabbed old women and threw them to the ground as they kicked and writhed in pain. In Novosibirsk, police sedated a hysterical woman with a needle, stabbing the shiny metal into her back. The provinces had joined the protests.

The people looted and pillaged my dachas. Agents hadn't reached them in time, or maybe they hadn't cared to. The people stole my possessions and virtually burned two dachas to the ground. By the time police had arrived at my Sochi cottage, only sheer curtains were left blowing in an open window. The people had turned against me.

Yet in Vidyayevo, home of the *Kursk*, there was silence. People were said to be at home, glued to their televisions which provided no information, clutching the remote, wishing for a break in programming. Or they prayed in the church, lighting candles and singing hymns of hope.

All I could manage was to walk to the door, open it and stand outside.

I stare at the unending leaves and the muddy ground. My cheek muscle starts to spasm.

The door opens. Gosha walks outside and stands beside me.

"Gospodin Putin, I have a message for you."

"What?"

"Bill Clinton is coming to Moscow."

The American President

A long-held secret, Bill Clinton had KGB connections.

He had visited the Soviet Union while a student in England, but only for eleven days.

He came around the holidays in 1969-70, which was five years before I entered the KGB. However, when he began campaigning for President of America, I'd heard all about his visit from my old KGB superior, Oleg Petrovich. He said Clinton acquired a visa with ease, a difficult task since Cold War tensions were high.

In those days, we didn't get many visitors from the West, only a brave few who stayed a couple of days at a nice hotel in Piter or Moscow then turned right around. They had the right to be scared. The streets were dirty, rife with corruption. The mafia loomed with their black purses, snatching percentages from all businesses, including the old ladies selling flowers on the street. Sophia Loren twirled around in Red Square while photographers clicked away and commoners gawked. She was the only excitement that had come to Moscow in 1969.

Clinton was supposed to stay in a cheap hostel infested with bed bugs and doors with locks that could easily be picked—and no heat. Blustery wind would barrel against the flimsy window pane. Oleg Petrovich received a call from one of the higher-ups to arrange a room at the Hotel National for an American named William Clinton. "He's on a train from Finland right now, due into Moscow in a couple of hours," the superior relayed, saving the future president from the miserable fate of an inner city hostel.

The KGB footed Clinton's entire hotel bill, Oleg Petrovich told me. I knew the Hotel National was reserved for those loyal to the Communist Party and ambassadors, so why had Clinton stayed there?

He was a lucky man, dodging the seedy digs of Moscow, handpicked for the swanky Hotel National. Back then, it was the place to be seen: thousands of rubles per room with gold-embossed curtains, grand pianos and marble bathrooms in every suite. The Hotel National was the opposite of communism. So for a Master's student living in England with a small stipend and no job, Clinton had to have done something to receive such attention from the Soviets. He'd been there for the War Moratorium, since he vehemently protested the Vietnam War.

Oleg Petrovich had picked up Clinton at the train station, and said the future American president was very nice to him. Clinton had a strange accent that he'd never heard before, even though his specialty was collecting information on dissidents from English-speaking countries. He asked Clinton where he was from. "Arkansas," he replied. Oleg Petrovich wasn't familiar with the place, assuming it was somewhere deep in the heartland of the United States. He said Clinton shook his hand and thanked him at all the appropriate times.

As they walked into the Hotel National, Clinton's face followed the gold vines and flowers that crept up the columns and ran wild all over the ceiling. He commented, "This sure is a nice place. The nicest hotel I've ever stayed in." Then Oleg Petrovich left him standing in the lobby with his nose pointed upwards.

Clinton attended the War Moratorium, listened and proposed his thoughts when asked. According to Oleg Petrovich, the KGB officials said Clinton was part hick, part hippie and dangerously intelligent, especially for an American from the South. When questioned by the KGB committee, Clinton answered with frankness. Then he launched into a small, sycophantic speech to appease all the Russians staring at him. Oleg Petrovich said that every one of the officers in that room remembered it for years afterward. It persisted in their heads.

They kept an open file on him, not as a dissident, but as someone to watch. The next time Clinton visited Moscow was when it was the Russian Federation. And he never revealed who paid for his entire stay, instead remaining a secret amongst the KGB family.

I hadn't seen Clinton since I was prime minister when we both attended a conference in New Zealand where he sat down next to me. We had a polite conversation through a translator for most of the meal. He said that he and his wife loved Moscow the last time they came, the architecture and cityscape, a few restaurants they liked. We discussed Russian history and how he enjoyed learning about the dynamic reformer Peter the Great.

He had done his research on me, since in previous interviews, I'd mentioned how Peter was one of my idols. I knew Clinton sat down next to me for a reason which I had yet to discover. He also was clever enough to avoid the unavoidable topic of Yeltsin, as opposed to other leaders who would ask me how he was doing, but with a smirk planted on their face. They took pleasure in the fact Russia failed because of Boris Yeltsin's embattlement with alcohol.

In the middle of the meal, he asked about Gospodin Yeltsin with a straight face.

Shifting in my seat, I said, "He's fine."

"Boris is quick on his feet and has a killer sense of humor."

He was referring to the press conference they'd held together in which Yeltsin called Clinton a "disaster." He laughed again as he retold the story. I smiled.

Clinton had a charm that I'd never experienced before. He had a photographic memory and conducted a great amount of research before meeting a person of importance. He spewed facts—both historical and personal—back at his subject. At the conference in New Zealand, he not only talked about Peter the Great, but about his poor upbringing in Arkansas. I admired his honesty.

As Clinton dissected his steak, he said to me, "You're the same as me, Vladimir. We both grew up in hard times."

I nodded my head in agreement after the translator switched his words into Russian.

"My life was not unlike yours in the Soviet Union. I mean, I struggled in my childhood. I wanted more. I always strove for more."

He chewed a piece of steak before I nodded again.

"I think in that way, Vladimir, we're the same person. Don't you think so?"

I nodded a third time at the rehearsed speech.

He laughed and said, "Well, Premier Putin, I think we're going to get along fine."

From those few words, I felt a sense of camaraderie as we rose from our seats. That meal had set the precedence for our working relationship. Clinton had intended it to go exactly that way. It was a good opportunity for me to see firsthand the inner workings of Clinton's mind, which weren't similar to mine, yet I understood them from studying the psychologies of people during my KGB days. He knew his place in the world, at the helm of the most powerful country on Earth, and for that, I had to admit I was a little jealous. But his charm and desire to relate to me and my people washed it away with pure admiration for the man.

When it was time to leave the room, the doors swung open to photographers waiting on the other side. Clinton and I emerged together, while he kept to the side of me, not a step in front. He shook my hand and smiled as the photographers snapped away.

Amerekanskee (American)

"What do you mean, 'Clinton is coming to Moscow'? Who invited him?"

Putin bristles at this prospect. Gosha doesn't want to explain the situation to his boss; however, he clears his throat and says the American president requested an impromptu meeting with Putin on his way back from China. He'd be at the Kremlin tomorrow. Gosha knows the next words out of his boss' mouth.

"I will think about it."

"Yes, Gospodin Putin."

Gosha has the usual task of dodging the Americans when they want an answer. Not a fun game to play. These people *demand*—everything must be done right now, right away and no excuses. And he can't use not understanding English as an excuse because he's fluent in the language. Perhaps the sole reason Putin chose him for the job, though he doubts it. Gosha had been taking international relations classes at university, and to be accepted into the required degree classes, he had to pass tests in English. That was the benefit of attending high school in Piter—he learned English from an early age, and in addition, he would listen to the English version of Radio Liberty when he couldn't sleep at night, or when he was bored. Speaking to the Americans or Brits was rare thus far, but when he did, he found the task quite easy.

Gosha can't wait for Clinton to visit Moscow. It would be his first big perk of the job, meeting the American president. He knows well enough to act stoic, like the visit doesn't matter, but on the inside, Gosha hopes for a framed photograph of he and Clinton, smiling and giving the thumbs up sign. Realistically, it won't happen. If Putin were to find out Gosha asked Clinton for a photo, he'd be fired on the spot.

Even more important, the boy hopes for a rescue crew for the *Kursk*. Would Clinton discuss the submarine explosion with Putin? Probably not. He doubts it because Clinton was already scheduled to talk with his Russian counterpart over the next couple of weeks anyway, about the pending missile defense shield and Iran.

Clinton's sudden visit to Moscow signifies urgent news from his China trip, more urgent than a foundering submarine.

A Wild Card

President Clinton looks forward to leaving the White House. Everything had gone swimmingly—the stimulated economy, the Internet boom, his growing popularity on the international stage.

Then she ruined his political career. And his personal life.

They had an arrangement, all of his aides knew. She would slip into the oval office at night and pleasure him any way he wanted. He would emerge with a smile on his face and sometimes his zipper unzipped. And his wife knew. She didn't exactly encourage it, but she knew, especially after the first time it happened. She had suspected as much this time around and demanded that he stop, more influenced by her political ambitions than his actual infidelity. He denied everything. So as usual, she froze him out.

They'd stopped having sex years ago, around the time their daughter was born. Clinton remembered the good old days, the fun wild sex, chasing his saran-wrapped wife around their first house. No kids or responsibilities. Just an afternoon romp in the hay any time he wanted. Then the kid came, and like many women do, she froze up, putting motherhood above any other priorities. Her vagina closed for business.

His options were limited. He couldn't divorce her. She'd be so brutal, he'd never see his child again. Divorce was out of the question. Separation was the next option, but at that time, he was on the path to governor, elected the following year. His campaign advisor strongly recommended against it. So he played along, pretending he loved his wife, pretending his marriage was wedded bliss. After a while, it became commonplace. He stopped caring, but surprisingly, she didn't. When she confronted him about the other woman, pain radiated from her green eyes. Vanilla-scented perfume wafted off her body as she waited for his answer. He looked away and denied the claim.

A few months later, the story hit the newspapers with the mistress holding all the evidence. She came forward lured by multimillion-dollar book deals from publishing houses and appearances on talk shows. News kept pumping in, trumping any important political matter of the day. The press salivated. William Clinton was now deemed a bad boy, a sex addict.

So he lied. He was advised to lie to the American people. To say it blew up in his face was an understatement. It nearly wiped him clean of all the hard work he had put in since childhood. Years of practice at drum line, model UN, the Ivy League college he attended. Years of throwing himself over his mother's small frame, shielding her from the oncoming blows of his father's drunken fists. Years of lying, learning to lie:

Tell your father you remembered to pick up a gallon of milk, William. Then go round back, run to the corner store, pick it up and come back here. He'll never know the difference. Please William. He won't know. He won't want the milk until after dinner with his coffee.

Billy, please don't tell Daddy. He'll hurt Momma. He'll hurt you.

You can exaggerate the truth, William. Colleges don't necessarily have to know it wasn't "Model UN" per se. They won't understand what Young Governors Club is. Just put down Model UN on the application.

You fucking piece of shit! Did you lie to me again, William Clinton? You didn't get the milk like I fucking asked! You ain't worth nothing. This whole fucking family is nothing. You know what, Billy? I'm going to tie you, no, I'm going to tie your balls to that mother fucking chair, and you're going to watch while I beat the living shit out of your momma. Get back here! Don't you run away from me!

The voices often haunted William Clinton as president of the United States. When he was a child, he used to put two pillows over his ears and rock back and forth, humming to himself. It terrified his little sister with whom he shared the same room. Actually, they shared the same bed; otherwise his father would come in the middle of the night and try to touch her. Once this behavior began, Clinton slept in the same bed with Sophie every single night, his arm wrapped around her. He thought it was inappropriate to sleep with his sister, but he was her only protection. Momma wasn't about to leave her husband who provided a decent source of income.

A reward for excellent marks and student leadership, he had the opportunity to meet the governor of the state at sixteen years old. He never went, lying, telling people he'd come down with an acute case of the flu. He couldn't bear to leave Sophie for one night although she begged him to go. A year later, some months before leaving for college, he bought Sophie a gun. Out back, in the field, he set up a shooting range and she practiced. Close-range, long-range. He installed a dead bolt on the bedroom door and locks on the windows. He found her a pit bull at a local shelter. He trained it to love them and hate their father.

Until Sophie went to college herself, far away and never returned home either, she remained safe in that rundown house. Sophie and the pit bull named Roxy.

Clinton tried very hard to get these memories out of his head. Sophie was a lawyer, all grownup and married with her own kids. His parents died several years ago. Momma in a car crash where a drunken driver—not his father—hit her head on. The impact ignited the car in flames, and dental records identified her body. His father died of massive liver failure.

"Mr. President, sir, the situation in Russia is getting worse."

Clinton pulls himself out his afternoon daydream and concentrates on his Secretary of State.

"How much worse?"

"We think it's a Gorbachev circumstance all over again."

"Is there a coup?"

"There are uprisings in all the major cities."

"Is another government being put in place?"

"We're not sure. Our inside sources are getting back to me on this."

"And the submarine?"

"That situation has not been solved either."

"Putin hasn't accepted international aid?"

"No. You know, President Putin. Mr. *Nyet.*"

"Alright then. Let's try to ask for a meeting one more time."

Clinton sits on the suede couch of a Beijing hotel. He looks into a crystal chandelier, which hangs over a mahogany dining room table, set with lit silver candelabras and extensive origami comprised of silk paper.

"It's a good thing you speak Russian, Secretary Albright."

"Yes, Mr. President. What message would you like me to pass on?"

"I'd really like to meet with him."

"He's in hiding, Mr. President. And Air Force One flying over—"

"We'll work out the details. I can talk with Putin, I'm sure of it."

"Yes, sir."

"Ask if he can meet on my way back to Washington tomorrow night. We'll reroute a little. We'll meet him near the Russian border, in the northwest. That won't be suspicious; we can land in Finland. I have a feeling he's in that vicinity anyway, especially if his wife and daughter are in Berlin. Hiding to the east doesn't make much sense."

"Yes, Mr. President."

"Remember to ask, Secretary Albright. He likes to be asked, not told."

"I will, Mr. President."

Back to the Kursk

Olya, Olen'ka. My dearest Olga. No, too formal. I only call her that when I want her attention in the grocery store. Olechka, that's my pet name for her—what I call her in the presence of others, and in bed. It's perfect.

The mind of Dima Kolesnikov ebbs and flows. Back and forth his consciousness drifts. His head feels loose on his neck and rolls as if his cervical spine has been severed and he's suffering from internal decapitation. Holding the pen in his uninjured hand becomes more of a burden, since it now weighs the size of a brick. He holds it tighter in his fist and thinks about what to write. It must be short, Dima can't write for long, and it must be poignant. Most importantly, it must be found so Olga understands what happened and why it happened, and then she can share the sailors' story with the living.

Through the haze, he sees a sailor moving his foot. He thought it was only him who has the unfortunate fate of staying alive.

We're dying in an undignified way. He wishes he has the strength and resources to clean the vomit dripping from his shirt. The pile of excrement solidifies into dried out, ice chunks under his buttocks. Once his brain cells start to die off, he will slip into the blackness and then his vital organs will start to fail one by one.

A while ago, he was upset, actually working up a good cry for the fact his life will end. But now, all he wants is to garner the endurance to write and let his body die. *Please let my body die if you have any mercy.*

He begins to write with an unsteady hand:

To my dearest Olechka,
I am writing blindly. The light in this compartment has dimmed to an insufferable level, but at least, it's mostly dry. From my first note, you should know what happened to us by now—the explosions, then the twenty-three of us who crawled into this compartment to wait for our rescuers. I don't know how long we've been trapped down here, several hours or days, I think.

I'm writing this note to tell you how much I enjoyed being your husband, if only for a short time. I still can't believe you married me, a poor sailor who drank too much.

Do you remember our second date, the metro ride in Piter? How the train stopped suddenly and I grabbed you around your jacket collar to keep you from falling? I almost laugh when I think of that now. The look on your face of sheer terror, a look that said: What am I doing with this man? We stopped seeing each other after that, and I was heartbroken, even though we'd only gone on two dates. But I called and called and finally we were married, the happiest day my life will ever see.

Please do not despair. I am not leaving you in sadness. I am leaving you in happiness. As we parted ways at the train station in Murmansk, I cried and cried in your arms. I couldn't bear the thought of leaving my beautiful wife. I'd never reacted to a mission like that before, maybe it was an omen. You stroked my head and whispered reassuring thoughts in my ear. You loved me the way a woman is supposed to love her husband. I can only hope I returned the sentiment.

Please say goodbye to my beloved mother and father. Tell my mother that I love her very much. Tell my father that he would've been proud of all twenty-three of us down here and not to be angry with the navy. And Sasha, my little brother, tell him to remain strong, to continue on his naval path to becoming a captain one day.

My lovely Olechka, you will have a good life. Stay with your mother in Piter for a while. This will help clear your head. It's better than remaining in our dreary flat, especially with the cold weather approaching next month.

I love you.

Dima

Vidyayevo

Another sleepless night awaits Roman and Irina. They lie in Sasha's large bed in his Vidyayevo flat. Roman has run out of sleeping pills for Irina; later today he'll make a trip to the pharmacy to buy some more. He isn't sure there'll be any left, since he assumes, like his family, the rest of Vidyayevo isn't sleeping either. He's had bouts of insomnia before, if he was nervous before a new submarine mission or worrying about finances, but he hadn't ever gone two full days and nights without sleep.

"I can't do this much more, Ira."

"Do what?"

"Not sleep."

"Welcome to my life. A mixture of migraines and insomnia. Pills for everything."

"It's nice of Sasha to give us his bed. The couch out there doesn't look comfortable."

"He's a good son."

"Yes, he is."

They both grow silent, thinking of their other son, who's good too.

"Irinka, you have to try to get some sleep."

"Impossible."

"Try."

"Roma, you know when you 'try' to sleep, sleep never comes. Impossible."

"Then let's try to stay awake. Then we'll get sleepy."

"That doesn't work either."

Roman rolls over, taking the covers with him.

As Irina yanks them back to her side, she says, "I feel a two-week bout coming on. Two weeks of no sleep. Last time this happened, it was right after the miscarriage."

In normal circumstances, Irina wouldn't dare to bring up this tragedy because the hurt from Roman's face is so visceral, it makes her cry. But another child is probably dead. And she's numb. Very numb.

"Please, Ira, don't. Not right now. I can't talk about the miscarriage."

"Do you think Dima is dead?"

To Roman, his wife's voice is a hollowed out tree.

"I honestly don't know anymore. I'm tired of guessing."

"I'm not. I think he's dead. There, I said it. Our son is fucking dead."

"Please, Ira, don't do this—"

Her body springs straight up. "Don't do what? Don't do what? DON'T DO WHAT?!"

She starts to do something so strange. Roman has never seen his wife do this before. She howls like a wolf.

Sasha runs into the room. He sees his mother in her nightclothes, sitting up in bed, howling. He stops and watches her, a feral animal, letting out her emotion. Roman gets out of bed without any regard for his wife and sits on the living room couch.

Sasha kneels down next to Irina. He puts his hand on the shoulder of her worn-out nightgown.

"Mama, it's okay. I'm here. It's Sasha. I'm here. Please stop howling."

She shuts her mouth.

"That's good, Mama. Thank you."

As he pets her hair, he says, "Mama, please lie down. I'm going to have a doctor come see you. It's okay. Just lie there quietly."

He pulls the covers over his mother and returns to the living room. Roman sits on the couch, elbows on his thighs, head in his hands.

"She's losing her mind."

"Yes, Papa, she is. I'm calling the doctor right now."

"Sasha?"

"Yes, Papa?"

Roman—beyond tired, overweight, old—looks at his son and says, "I can't take this anymore."

Olga

Olga curls up in a ball under the living room table which holds the TV. She's been there for many hours. She's cried enough tears to drown a U-boat. To pass the time, she watches her hungry cat, back arched in concentration, gnaw the legs of the sofa. It crunches on the wood chips and swallows them down to its supple stomach. A few minutes later, the cat will regurgitate them as if coughing up a hairball. Olga watches this cycle over and over because, somehow, it comforts her.

Help

"Gospodin Putin, we've received a second offer of international aid. From the Norwegians and the Brits. They'll provide a rescue vehicle and divers."

"For free?"

"For a price, of course."

"Of course," I mumble.

"Gospodin Putin, time is running out. A decision has to be made. Do we accept aid or not?"

"Igor Dmitrievich, I thought you and Popov were against accepting aid. Why the sudden change?"

Sergeyev sighs. "Well, Vladimir Vladimirovich, there's no way we can save them. We don't have the divers or the equipment. It's impossible. The only way to save the sailors is to accept aid. I don't like it—neither does Popov—but what choice do we have? Russia is crumbling all around us."

"Tell them thank you, but no thank you."

He sighs again. "Yes, Gospodin Putin."

I hang up the phone. Even though protests raged, I can't expose our military defense. Sixteen years in the KGB taught me to protect Mother Russia, to never let another country see her vulnerable. My instinct is to keep protecting her, this time at the cost of 118 men. I'm trying to make the best decision for the country and the Russian people. But I'm coming off as heartless, when in reality, I'm thinking about the best outcome for everyone involved. Why can't they see that?

I look around the hideout. A secret service agent stands at the door. He stares out to the living room, but a second ago, I could've sworn he was staring at me and listening to my phone conversation.

I'm helpless. Only my fifteen-year-old daughter has my best interests in mind. Maybe Gosha too. I can't do this alone. I can't take back Russia by myself. I need help. I need Bill Clinton.

December 1969

The train chugged along the tracks from Stockholm, where young William Clinton had the good fortune of taking a seat next to a voluptuous Swedish siren. One the sexiest women he'd ever seen. Driven by his penchant for blonds, he sweet-talked her into staying at his hostel. The evening ended with Ingrid—that was her name—blowing him in between bong hits on the rickety bed of an immaculate hostel room.

Drinking was not William Clinton's vice. Smoking pot back in his youth helped him become more social. In undergrad he was known as a stiff, the most boring freshman on campus. His roommate introduced him to the magical healing powers of the bong, allowing him to forget that Sophie was all alone back in Arkansas, that his father terrorized his mother. The ganj wiped his mind clean. He took his studies seriously though. He'd earned a full scholarship. And he couldn't fuck with that.

Girls became a new fascination. They were all over the place, and not anything like the prissy southern belles. These girls put out at every opportunity. Alcohol wasn't necessary to persuade them. The Northeast girls liked to have sex, to party before marriage. Sunday through Wednesday, he studied very hard, aided by the help of his photographic memory. He'd read a book once to memorize its entire contents.

Once hump day came on Wednesday night, he took the expression literally and turned the middle of the week into an all night, 1960s fuck fest. Sometimes, he, his friends and the girls took the party into the woods, like a bunch of New England prep school kids, and built bonfires, drank, smoked and fornicated all night long. It was nice to get away from family problems and studies. Clinton never had the opportunity before to be so free, so spirited and without any consequences to others. He was not in the protector role; he was not in the scared child role. He could party, he could work, he could do both equally and accomplish his dreams. Sophie would be out of the house in a couple years and he could get a good job and send money to her at college.

Then he moved to London after graduation, far away from his sister, who was attending an all women's college in the New England area. During his first year of studies, he grew tired of touring Western Europe; he'd been all over Great Britain, France, Italy. The unknown, darkly veiled Eastern Europe called his name. Clinton booked tickets during the Christmas break, a three-week trip from East Germany up to Sweden then Finland and finally a train to Moscow, his last stop. Then he'd fly back to London. He thought of taking a friend, but he yearned to do this alone. No compromises.

The murky waters of the Helsinki port froze into a translucent glacier. As he peered through the camera lens, Clinton decided not to take the photo. December, right after Christmas 1969, in faded bell bottoms and donning dark sideburns, Clinton put the camera down and turned his face into his coat to deflect the whipping wind of the Baltic Sea. It was his last photo before he was to head to the train station for a long, exhausting fifteen-hour ride from Helsinki to Moscow. He couldn't wait. He had all of his papers in order, ready to go where many Americans hadn't gone before: the Soviet Union.

He was supposed to stay in a cheap hostel in Moscow, one he'd booked months ago. That morning, he received a call from a man with a heavy Russian accent. "Another man will meet you at the train so stay on the platform." And he hung up. Clinton never expected his connection to come through *and* find him in a hostel in the middle of Helsinki, Finland.

He boarded the train, handing his ticket to a polite Finnish conductor who spoke perfect English. In a robotic Scandinavian voice, the man said they'd been told to watch out for him because his cabin had been upgraded to the first class compartment. The conductor escorted him to the front of the train and pulled open the door. Clinton scanned the cabin. So this is first class? The compartment had two pull-down beds situated up high. Two hard benches, smelling of lemon cleaner, were below. The Finn opened the bench for young William, showing him where to store his things. The picture window was large. He could look out, observing the landscape as the train rolled into the Soviet Union.

"Passport, please."

"You want me to give you my passport?"

"Yes. It's standard procedure. So nothing gets stolen. It's for your protection."

Clinton reached inside of his jacket and grabbed the passport and documents out of his pocket and handed them over.

"We lock them up and redistribute them once we get to the border."

"And then you lock them up again?"

"Yes."

The stupidity of Europe. Living in Western Europe, there was a lot of stupidity too, doing things for no reason at all, because they were "the system." He'd learned to acquiesce.

"Have a good trip. I will check on you later."

He stood there for a second. Clinton didn't know if he should tip so he dipped his hand into his pants pocket and rustled around for a few Finnish markka. He pulled out a fresh bill, straight from the exchange place, and stuck it out. The conductor stared at the money then at Clinton and walked away.

Left standing there for a second, Clinton finally registered what'd happened, shook his head and chalked up the odd exchange to a cultural difference. He'd been there a couple days, but he already knew the Finns were weird.

He sat down on the bench, facing the front of the train so he wouldn't get motion sickness. A few minutes later, the train began its slow chug. The excitement returned. In a matter of hours, he'd be in the Soviet Union, in Russia, a place so far from his rural Arkansas home. As a child Russia was in his nightly dreams. He didn't care what people said, calling him a commie lover, a pinko. It was a faraway place with onion dome cathedrals of brilliant shapes and colors, history around every corner.

The train gained speed. Finland whisked by. Once it got to full speed, he wouldn't be able to look out the window, sickened by the flickering images. He had a lot of time to think.

Sophie was good. Dating a boy, a nice boy he heard from his mother. She went to visit Sophie without their father for fall break. Clinton sent her the money to take a train up from Little Rock to outside of Boston. Sophie said it was the best Thanksgiving she'd ever had, no drama whatsoever, having a calm meal with her mother, the new boyfriend and his family. Mama must've been nervous, those fancy New England people. She must've been quiet the entire meal.

Several hours later the train stopped and another conductor, a Russian man, returned with Clinton's passport and documents. But he didn't leave like the Finn. He remained until the border guards came crashing onto the train. Doors thrown open, high-pitched laughing, slurred Russian. Vodka, similar to his father's, worked its way into the compartment before he saw the guards. Then they appeared. Two young men stumbling, giggling, unshaven. Once they saw Clinton, their faces molded into snarls.

"Passport and documents," one said in Russian.

Clinton understood what they meant.

One ripped the papers out of his outstretched hand and opened to the smiling passport photo. They erupted into hysterics. The conductor rolled his eyes. The men kept laughing, hardly reading the information on the documents. Then the laughing halted as they both caught sight of something on the paper. They pointed and looked up. They shoved the passport and documents back at Clinton, nodded and quickly moved on to the next passenger. The conductor eyed him and walked away, shutting the compartment door and forgetting to collect the passport and documents for safe keeping.

The papers went back into his jacket pocket. Clinton decided to pull down the bed and get some sleep, around ten hours to Moscow. He could get plenty of rest and then spend the evening in Red Square, walking around the city, gazing at the spectacular cathedrals.

Before he knew it, awoken out of a sound sleep, the train whistled and stopped. Clinton, groggy-eyed, sat up and looked out the window at the Moscow train station. He pushed aside the coat he used as a cover, jumped down from the bed and threw on his warm clothes to combat the bitter cold. He grabbed his things and left the train.

Out on the platform, he was about to rush to the hostel when he stopped in his tracks. The instructions. Wait on the platform.

Scanning the area, he didn't see anyone out of the ordinary. How was he supposed to tell his Russian from all the other Russians? They all looked the same—fur hat, heavy black coat, black pants, black shoes, a cigarette propped between chapped lips.

Clinton stood there, freezing, wishing that he'd taken the time to pull on long underwear. His teeth chattered. The train station was one long concrete platform, in an outside half-shell. The train he rode in on looked the nicest out of all them. Brakes squealed, in desperate need of oil. The women stepping down the platform covered their heads with babushka scarves and used plastic bags for luggage. Basic knowledge of Cyrillic allowed Clinton to read the Russian signs placed in the train windows. Valga/Valka. Narva/ Ivangorod. Where were these places?

A sensation that he was being watched flooded over him. Out of his peripheral vision, he saw a man at the other end of the platform. When Clinton caught sight of him, the man started to walk. Clinton did the same. Both of the men, trains arriving and departing to the left and right, marched down the grey concrete. As the man got closer, young William could see he had on the same outfit as everybody else. He jammed his hands into his pockets. His features were wooden, like all oppressed people of the Eastern bloc. He walked until he and Clinton were face to face.

The American stuck out his hand, smiling, and said to the Russian, "Hi, I'm William Clinton."

The man stared at the hand. Clinton's face flushed, not understanding again if he made yet another faux pas. A hand then reached out to shake his. The face did not smile.

"I know who you are," said the man in a heavy Russian accent.

"But I don't know who you are," Clinton said, laughing at his own unfunny joke.

They dropped hands. Clinton's laughing turned into a prolonged cough. The man watched the awkwardness until he stopped coughing.

"I am Oleg."

"Nice to meet you, Oleg. You can call me Bill. That's what everyone calls me."

Shut up! Shut up! Clinton's inner logic screamed. Nervousness made him jabber on. On rare occasions, he'd meet someone who allowed him to talk himself into idiocy. The other person who had this effect on him was a Polish professor from last term. Clinton met with him in office hours to discuss the theme of his economics paper. The professor let him yammer on, staring the whole time. No nodding or words of agreement, just a cold stare and when he finished his nonsense, the professor said, "Sounds fine."

"Follow me."

Clinton's logic kicked in; he did not respond, he followed. His smile disappeared, since it attracted attention. The people around him gaped at the lone smiling guy in the train station. They would be robbed in two

seconds if Clinton didn't get it together. This wasn't America. He had to
assimilate. He turned down the corners of his mouth. He pulled the coat
around him, thankful that he'd chosen a black coat months ago, and tugged
the American-looking ski hat down on his head. The bell bottoms had to be
stashed away the minute he arrived at his accommodations. He'd change into
everything black.

As they walked out of the station, a mob of ice skaters glided in front.
Small children teetered, holding the hands of their mothers. Clinton stepped
onto the street, nearly slipping on the slick ice, realizing why it doubled as
an outdoor ice rink. To his right was a vast expanse of white snow piled in a
park. Cross-country skiers followed a carved out path, doing classical or skat-
ing style, the latter much prettier.

The wind smacked Clinton's face. He pulled his hat down more and
his collar over his neck. He stood and watched the scene in front of him. All
of these Russians, in black and some in grey, spinning, weaving, gliding and
turning in circles. Some even laughing.

"Continue to follow me."

Oleg caught the American being a tourist. He turned around to retrieve the young man. Clinton followed, continuing to look back.

As they walked, William got on the sidewalk. Oleg steered him next
to the building, not under the edge of the awning. One of the few things he
mumbled on their walk was that icicles fell once in a while and killed people.
Similar to all the other pedestrians, they hugged each building.

The walk lasted twenty minutes or so. Clinton was so focused on Oleg,
he barely had time to look around. He observed a lot of red brick, cobblestone
and street signs on the sides of buildings instead of on poles like where he
was from. They crunched through the snow, his boots getting more and more
soaked. He assumed Oleg would pick him up in a car or a taxi and drop him
off. He hadn't guessed a hurried walking tour of Moscow. The man had to
get back to work.

Finally they arrived at their destination. He'd been so consumed in
avoiding a fallen icicle that Clinton hadn't noticed they were in the heart of
Red Square. Oleg looked left and right and walked across the street. Clinton
did the same. The building they were walking toward couldn't be the small
hostel he booked, for around $2 a night. The façade epitomized superiority,
luxury, history—ornate stone carvings on the top and bottom of each elon-

gated window, the crisp, newly-painted peach exterior, the building so massive—this wasn't Soviet at all.

A doorman held open the door and nodded to Oleg then to Clinton. In the lobby two huge statues of naked men with cloths to cover their nudity framed a doorway. They reminded Clinton of the Venus di Milo, though all body parts in tact, combined with Jesus on the cross. On a marble column in the corner, gold vines and flowers crept upwards and ran wild all over the ceiling.

"Where are we?"

Oleg came beside him. "The Hotel National."

"You mean where Lenin lived?"

"Yes. You are staying here."

"This is sure a nice place. The nicest hotel I've ever stayed in."

Clinton snapped out of his reverie of decadence once he heard the words slip out of his mouth. And in that damn Southern accent he tried to hide, even auditing a vocal class his freshman year in his undergrad. Sometimes he slipped into Southern mode. It was rare anymore, but when his defenses were down or he was too relaxed or generally not thinking, the twang came rushing out of his mouth. He knew Oleg heard every word because the man shot him a strange look.

"Yes. I will pick you up at eleven tomorrow morning to attend the War Moratorium. You should prepare a speech."

"Excuse me?"

"You understand why you're here, Mr. Clinton?"

"Maybe I don't. I had a connection in the Russian government who I thought was going to show me around a little, maybe help upgrade me to a better hostel. But all this, I don't know."

Oleg began to walk to the front desk. "Time to check in, Mr. Clinton."

"But what am I doing here, what War—"

"This woman is ready to check you in. The bellhop will take your bags to your room. I'll be back tomorrow morning."

December 1969 Continued

Men crowded into the War Moratorium. Clinton walked into the room. He didn't look nervous, but the debilitating cigarette smoke made him wince. He had smoked some reefer that he'd bought from the bellhop at the hotel. Eyes bloodshot, feeling the mellow, he was ready for the Moratorium. He'd organized one earlier that year at his school, leading the protest against the Vietnam War.

He sat down on the wooden chair next to Oleg Petrovich.

Clinton wore all black. Black pants, shirt, shoes, socks. He shaved off the sideburns, but kept the thick mustache because it was popular in Moscow. His lean frame contrasted against the vodka-soaked bellies of middle-aged Russian men. Maybe they weren't middle-aged. Eastern Europeans aged faster than any other people he'd ever seen. He could've sworn the bellhop was forty when in fact he'd just celebrated his twentieth birthday.

Yellowing, hound dog faces eyed Clinton, who shifted in his chair.

Removing the cigarette from his mouth, the Moratorium leader said something to Clinton. Oleg translated, "Tell us why you protest the Vietnam War so actively."

"Thank you for having me here today," he started as he sat up straighter. Oleg translated after him.

"I apologize for my lack of Russian. But I can read the street signs if you'd like me to."

Clinton cracked a smile, expecting laughter. Stern countenances continued to stare him down. His jokes were lost on this crowd. *Must be lost in translation?*

"The War has disrupted my country. I believe it's unwise to fight in a country where we have no business fighting. The people, the men of my generation are losing lives to a senseless war. We are reacting to our fear of communism."

Men stirred in their seats.

"We lost North Korea to communism. Then Vietnam. In the US, we don't believe in your system of communism and it's a feared word among our citizens. But I feel, personally, that even though we do not want this political system for ourselves, we should let other countries decide their own fate. And now we're losing fathers, brothers, sons. From my high school alone, a tiny town in the southern US, I know of twenty young men, my age, who have lost their lives in this war. It must stop."

"Why are you not a soldier? You're a young, healthy man. Did you dodge conscription?"

"No. You're not drafted when you're in school. I've been underage, then when I turned eighteen I was already headed to university. And now I'm in school in England, as you know."

"Any final comments?"

"I respect Russia. It's been a dream of mine to come here ever since I was a small child. At the library, I would borrow books on your czars, the onion dome cathedrals. I'd imagine walking in Red Square as I turned the pages of my book. Traveling took me away to another place, away from the problems of home life. Not all Americans are what you see on the television. Many are fascinated by this unknown country, wishing they had the opportunity to visit as well. However, the War separates and distances us from one another and that's a shame."

You could hear a pin drop at the Moscow War Moratorium of 1969.

"You may leave."

"Thank you," said Clinton as he got up and left, the eyes of at least 100 men following him all the way out the door.

William Clinton assumed they were government agents, and they were, but ones of the KGB. They'd been following his student protests in England through the eyes of a "Polish" university professor who remarked he had a Master's student particularly interested in Russia. And he was bright enough to pick up the language. A potential collaborator, a potential source?

To observe more of Clinton, they added a student to his classes, registered in international policy who could mimic an authentic English accent. Per his superiors' instructions, he wasn't too friendly with Clinton, but cordial enough to offer him his "contact" in the Russian government when the American mentioned he wished to travel there for winter break. After class, he handed Clinton a paper with an address. "Write him a letter. You can probably get a better hotel out of it or something. Get you out of your dodgy accommodations." Clinton thanked him, wrote the letter and never heard back.

Then the phone rang at the hostel in Helsinki that morning—the terrifying Russian system of communication, he'd assumed. Until he met Oleg, he hadn't an idea of his acquaintance's contact. He figured out after the KGB agent left him in the lobby, he was being exploited for another purpose and for the sake of returning to England alive, he'd go along with the process. The only way he could escape safely but follow through was to act like a screw up. He'd never attended a protest high before, but if smoking would get him out of this mess, he'd do it. He devised a plan: he'd buy the ganj from the bellhop and smoke it with him. Hell, he was probably a spy too.

The plan worked in Clinton's favor. The KGB agents were impressed by his passionate speech and reverence for the Motherland and its political undertakings, but not impressed with the idea of a hippie under their direction. They'd heard about the fruitcake American hippies, so out of their minds and dissident, high all the time, sloppy and whining. With cigarettes in one hand, the KGB voted "yes" or "no" with the other. Did they want Clinton in their circle? The overwhelming answer was *nyet*. Clinton could stay one more night at the Hotel National for his love of Mother Russia and then be relegated to a decent hostel a couple kilometers from Red Square.

Clinton received a call from Oleg Petrovich the next morning; the rest of his stay would be at a reputable hostel on the outskirts of Red Square. The American had won the game. He breathed a sigh of relief upon hanging up the phone and collapsed into the velvet chair and picked up the phone again. He called to the front desk asking for the bellhop to help with his bags. He had two pieces of manageable luggage and over an hour until he had to leave, but he wanted to see if the man was selling more marijuana. The Russian herb wasn't very good, but it was there and for now, it would suffice.

Clinton in Narva

Goddamn, I was fucked up that morning. Clinton thinks about how he stumbled out of the Hotel National, tripping over his own two feet, the bellhop holding him up by the shoulder and shoving him out the door.

He's on his way to meet Putin in Estonia. He's never been to Estonia before, but he's heard about it. He knows the Estonian President, Lennart Meri, hates Putin. Back when Putin was prime minister, he and Meri attended a European Union conference. In a speech to EU heads of state, Meri called Russians "occupiers" and Putin retaliated by getting up and stomping across the marble floor. He let the metal door bang on his way out. He was a real hero to the Russians for standing up to Meri, but ever since then, they despised each other.

Clinton and his staff flew into Kotka, Finland, an overall boring layover. Though he hasn't smoked in over twenty-five years, he likes a good time while on vacation. But he has to keep his nose clean now. Any clandestine trips to a strip club or strippers brought in from outside, or a gorgeous, young Eastern European woman brought to his bedroom, waiting naked upon his arrival, is a thing of the past. Just six months until the presidency ends and he could do whatever the hell he wants. He and his wife have a verbal agreement—he'd help her politically and she'd look the other way at his indiscretions. Yet she'd found a way to keep tabs on him at all times; she'd already bought a house in the suburbs of Columbus, Ohio, filled with young families and nothing but porky, Midwestern soccer moms. He was looking forward to the slim, in-shape physiques of the city women, assuming they'd be moving to the powerhouse Democratic state of New York. In the end, she wanted Ohio. Back to porker-ville. But he doesn't mind going hogging once in a while, as long as it's good hogging.

Clinton countered his wife's decision by obtaining office space in downtown Columbus, bordering the area near the drug dealers and the start of gentrification. He bought a whole floor, speaking with the architect about building an apartment with half of the space—in case he has to spend some late nights there. He doesn't mind the gunfire as long as he isn't trapped like a prisoner in his own house.

After they land in Kotka, he boards a hydrofoil at the port. It takes less than an hour to get to Narva, a smooth ride across cobalt waters. The orange haze of the setting sun spills onto the front window of the boat, warming Clinton as he nibbles on the buffet of reindeer meat, black bread and cold cuts. He cuts a piece of meat, tender and moist, and puts it in his mouth. It's good, like nothing he's tasted before, but good.

His staff told the Finnish government President Clinton needed rest in a Kotka hotel before continuing on to Helsinki. He had to be brought in privately. The American ambassador to Finland already made arrangements for Clinton to make a morning speech. Confused, the Finnish government asked the contents of the speech to which the ambassador replied, "I don't know." Curiosity burned in the minds of the Finns, wanting to know why Clinton is stopping over—it must be important. In the end, they don't care. He's a celebrity and he's always welcome, putting their country on the map.

Clinton arrives at the Narva port, on the west bank of the Narva River. He steps off the hydrofoil onto the dock, which arches and levels like a Chinese dragon. A small breeze floats over the water onto Clinton's face. Black trees silhouette the indigo sky. The moon lights up the haggard faces of the dockworkers. A large company has been discussing a ferry line for tourists from Narva to Kotka for a couple years, but the powers that be haven't made any business deals. In both countries, the people hoped for this opportunity to create more jobs, but in reality, who would want to vacation in either of these places when St. Petersburg is so close?

Fortunately for Clinton and his staff, the Finnish and Estonian ambassadors get along, the former making a phone call to the latter explaining that Clinton desired to see the earthquake's destruction in Narva. To see if the US could help. The Estonian ambassador was so flattered, he ecstatically said "yes" to allowing a quiet trip there. *The US is coming to help. We'll be accepted in the EU. We'll be accepted now!*

A call to President Meri confirms the ambassador's impulsive answer. After Meri hangs up the phone, he finds it suspicious that Clinton would rearrange his trip to check on minimal destruction in a virtually unknown country. The US has never cared about Estonia before, why now? Meri shrugs and sits back in his chair. He's watching the first cut of the documentary he made before becoming president. He hopes to have it mass marketed by next year.

Milaya (My Cherished)
August 16, 2000 Wednesday midnight

"Mashenka, go to bed. I'll be back soon."

"Where are you going, Papa?"

"To a meeting."

"With whom?"

"President Clinton."

"Really?"

"Yes, Masha. Now go to bed."

"Where's the meeting?"

"Right across the border. In Estonia."

"But President Meri hates you."

I raise my eyebrows.

"Stay here, Mariya."

"Yes, Papa."

"And don't talk about this meeting with secret service. They know, but it's best not to—"

"I get it, Papa. I'm not stupid."

I pat her on the head. As I am about to leave the bedroom, I turn around and glance at my daughter. We lock eyes. She seems as if she's taking a snapshot of me with her memory. I can almost hear the click of the shutter inside her brain as she nods. I nod back and shut the door behind me.

The Bridge

Clinton cannot cross over the border so Putin has to, with the help of a secret service agent who went to gymnasium with the head of the Estonian border patrol. Putin sits in the car at the end of the bridge and waits as the agent and patrolman drink vodka and reminisce about their childhood.

The agent says to his friend, "We're going to Narva, looking for some pussy."

After an inebriated hiccup, the friend slaps his back and says, "Ha! I knew you weren't faithful to your wife."

"Not for me, for some friends. Just to hang out. We're stuck here in Ivangorod, bored. Might as well make a good time of it."

"Why not!"

The friend tells him the name of a prostitute who works at the train tracks. Lana charges fifty kroons for a blowjob, but she has scabs on the corners of her mouth. Or there is Anya who is young and beautiful and her door is always open, but she comes at the high price of 400 kroons. The security officer takes Anya's address and slips it in his pocket.

"I'm going to get my friends now."

Putin sits in the back of the car next to Gosha; three security officers sit in the front and one in the back—all dressed in plain clothes. Six men to a car give the appearance of friends on a bachelor mission. The only disguise the President wears is a newsboy hat, since it's night and the border patrol will let them pass.

The car glides over the unbroken pavement of the bridge. They come to a dead stop at the border patrol about to enter Narva. The security officer's window rolls down.

The patrolman sticks his head in. Putin holds his breath.

"Just wanted to see who's fucking Anya tonight."

The agent's shaking finger points to Gosha.

The friend seizes up the boy with a swaying head. He slurs, "Good luck, young man!"

Putin continues to stare into his lap, the brim of the cap covering the recognizable features of his face.

Security rolls up the window. The friend bangs his hand twice on the metal roof and Putin is on his way to meet President Clinton.

Mikhail

"Another phone call from Boris Berezovsky, Mr. President."

"Again?"

"Yes, Mr. President. And there is one call from Mikhail Khodorkovsky."

Clinton laughs. He won't be answering that call. Khodorkovsky has been calling him for a while now, even trying to go through former President Bush to arrange a meeting. Clinton would rather be water boarded than talk to Khodorkovsky. To him, the oligarch is very intelligent, but untrustworthy. He calls himself "democratic" and "liberal," but Clinton has yet to see these qualities in him. Instead, he sees a power-hungry Russian and a communist.

The Communist Party groomed Khodorkovsky, and all of his affiliations lead back to it. There's no way he would bite the hand that fed him for so many years. In other words, Clinton thinks that if Khodorkovsky takes over, Russia will take a step back into some form of communism and then Vice President Gore, who will hopefully win the presidency in November, will have to deal with another Cold War. He doesn't want that legacy for Gore, or for himself. It's been a long eight years, with his name dragged through the mud. At the very least, he can end his presidency on a good note with Russia.

Enter Putin. Clinton sees him as his Russian counterpart. He came from nothing, and he worked his way up to the presidency. Putin is stoic, cold and unrelenting. He loves control. But Clinton thinks he's workable, despite his KGB image and tough exterior. After researching and observing him for some time now, Clinton has come to the conclusion that Putin likes money. He likes capitalism, and that's where Clinton has the upper hand. Nothing in this world has a chance at capitalism if it's not American-backed. Putin needs the US, especially now.

"We're almost at the meeting spot, Mr. President."

Hanging Post

August 16, 2000 Very early morning

We pull into an opening in the forest. The car sputters and stops. I get out, while Clinton's motorcade hovers around us. I look around, but can't find Clinton. His secret service team is comprised of black men who look like they've been pumped with a super hormone. They resemble American football players, but in polished suits and earpieces.

One approaches me. He is so black, the whites of his eyes and teeth glow.

"President Putin, President Clinton will be here any minute."

Four cars precede Clinton and he's in none of them. Here I am, pulling up in an average vehicle, crammed in the back with my aide and a secret service agent.

I nod to the agent, understanding the basics of what he says. Gosha will be my translator with the President. The only highlight of his pathetic resume was he speaks English.

The agent instructs another agent to stay with him and for the others to inspect the surrounding area. My secret service, who hardly speak English, work in cooperation with the Americans, although they're outnumbered by Clinton's men.

I concentrate on relaxing my face as best as I can. If not, that humiliating cheek spasm would return and Clinton would have an unabridged reading of my thoughts. In judo, I center my emotions on the outcome, how I perceive the last throw of my opponent to get the win. This proves a more difficult task than I've imagined because I don't know Clinton's motive in arranging this meeting.

"Are you alright, Gospodin Putin?" Gosha asks.

"Fine."

But I'm not. I begin to walk across the field in search of an answer, in search of something out there that would aid me. The sound of rushed voices grows faint, the mobiles, the agents, they all went away. I walk deeper into the field until I see a clear picture of my father's past.

The rotting wood is sawed to perfection. The structure has sharp edges at the perpendicular angle of the where the wood pieces meet. Abandoned by Nazi soldiers long ago, the frayed ropes, worn out from so much torture, are nonexistent. I stand underneath the hanging post. The wind blows as an invisible entity swings to and fro over my head. It has to be a child, since there's not enough space for an adult. I look up, imagining the purplish, frostbitten feet dangling with snarling toenails and fungus loitering underneath the nail bed. I shouldn't be affected by this. I was KGB after all. I had witnessed torture many times before. Oleg Petrovich asked dissidents to stick their heads into the built-in funnel in the stone wall, and when the fit was snug, he shouted a command and a gun fired on the other side of the wall. The bullet sliced through the dissident's brain. My superiors had no choice but to perform those executions—they protected the state. The Nazis, on the other hand, executed without mercy.

I reach out to touch the splintered hanging post. I think of SS soldiers and the job they signed up for, exterminating men, imprisoning men like Papa. If I had to, I would've killed them all with mercy. Compassion does dwell in the recesses of my mind, unused for awhile. It thrashed around louder and louder, bringing me to hire Gosha, for all of his awkwardness and lack of sensibility, there was a moment in that interview, where I saw myself standing in front of my desk, trembling in a knock-off designer suit, desperate for a chance at a new life. I read the ridiculous resume and wondered why my staff had chosen him. Later, I found out it was an oversight on my secretary's part; in other words, the boy slipped through the cracks. But after meeting Gosha and observing his fright, I realized I could mold him into exactly what I aspired out of a personal aide. He came from a poor background like me, while the other candidates were sons of the oligarchs, or other wealthy Russians, who already had their lives planned out for them. On the other hand, Gosha was a challenge—in fact, he was a work in progress. But he wasn't a threat. He would keep his mouth shut because everything to him would be new and important. I raised many eyebrows selecting him, but as this chaos progresses, my choice remains loyal.

I glance at the watch tower menacing above the tree line. It soars, a wooden structure resembling Popsicle sticks glued next to each other to form the balcony. The sides have two wooden Xs as support beams. A black figure, a secret service agent I presume, walks back and forth, the light bulb of the moon behind him. If anyone sees him tonight, they'd swear they've seen a ghost from sixty years ago.

My life is a sinister reminder of the past, the struggle I had endured to be standing in this field. To some, I appear sadistic in nature. And part of me is; most people have a dark place that doesn't creep out in the open until it's necessary. As a little boy, thoughts came and went, as what happens with little boys in general, escaping the boredom of playgrounds for the thrill of dressing up as a soldier or spy. But what happened if that world was not a mere fantasy anymore—if it elapsed into reality, a life of fighting against the "bad guys"? And somewhere along the lines, people believed that you turned into the exact thing you were fighting? I went into the KGB with the best of intentions, the ambitious desire to elevate my economic and social status. The chance to fulfill a childhood dream. As often happens, that flawless, protected bubble of my dream world popped—being a KGB agent was a job. A boring job that consisted of signing crisp sheets of paper and ensuring they were delivered to the appropriate superior. And sixteen years later, I was stuck in Dresden, with a wife and two young daughters and nowhere to go. That was how the state repaid me for my unwavering devotion.

Clinton had experienced the same disappointment. He embraced luck throughout his presidency—a good economy, an Internet boom, no war. He rode it until he got caught. But all he did was have sex with a woman who wasn't his wife and he's paying for that mistake on a daily basis. Americans forgot about their comfortable houses and big salaries and focused on the mistake.

Clinton knows what it is to have no control of the people or his political career. He'd been humiliated, vilified and scorned. But he's still president.

Someone taps my shoulder.

I turn around to see the white strands of hair. He's so close to me that unidentifiable meat on his breath hits my face.

"Vladimir, it's good to see you again."

A flashlight illuminates the crow's feet which exaggerates his age and makes his eyes appear smaller than they are. The bags underneath match mine, except his aren't purple, but they're swollen. When Clinton had started the presidency, he had none of these marks of old age, and a tuft of dark brown hair. To see what eight years in office did to a person is depressing. I'd end my presidency the same way, with battle scars indenting my face for posterity.

He looks like Bill Clinton, but a worn out, burnt out, soon-to-be former president. Yet behind the lassitude, energy radiates from his hazel eyes.

"Vladimir, how are you?" Clinton says as he sticks out his hand.

Behind us, Gosha switches his words into Russian.

I shake his hand with force as it weakens in my grip. "Fine, President Clinton, I appreciate you being here."

He laughs. "President Clinton? You know me better than that, Vladimir. We go all the way back to New Zealand. Call me Bill, of course."

"Fine, Bill."

"Being a fugitive agrees with you. You look a hell of a lot better than I do."

"I haven't served my country for eight years."

"That's true. We'll walk and discuss everything. I'm dying for some exercise, I've been on planes for a couple days now. You know how that is."

I've forgotten how strange his accent is, the distinct on and off twang imbued through certain words, yet I don't understand much of what he says. Gosha continues to translate.

We start on a path that cuts through the forest, leaving the field of gallows behind. Clinton doesn't react to the hanging posts; he turns and walks away. Gosha follows, listening and translating, and holding a flashlight so that Clinton and I can see each other's faces. Meanwhile, from the area of the motorcade emerge a handful of agents. They surround us on every side, yet far enough away to not hear the conversation. My security joins them around the perimeters, in front and back to guarantee our safety.

Clinton comments, "A creepy thing, that tower. Can you imagine the brutality that happened here? Appalling."

Gosha stumbles over a word and says it in English.

"Creepy?" I repeat.

"Gives you chills, scares you. Creepy."

Gosha translates.

"Yes, okay."

"Can you imagine the brutality, Vladimir?"

"Yes."

"Do you know where we are?"

"An old concentration camp."

"It's called Vaivara. I looked it up while we were riding here; it was established as a Soviet prisoner camp, but, of course, Jews came through here."

I remain silent, thinking about my father as a soldier in World War II Narva. I never did find out how the Estonians saved him.

"Yes."

For a split second, he scrutinizes my face, an attempt to search beyond my outer expression of a solid statue and read into my answer. To him, it's more than a simple yes. Then he snaps his head forward.

"Tell me about your flights. Your trip to China and Finland," I force myself to ask.

The conversation would be best if we start off slowly. The American custom is to engage in small talk first. I find it to be a waste of time and energy, but now it's a useful device to sense Clinton's mood.

"China was nice. China is a hard country to deal with though, but you know that, Vladimir. A little stubborn they are," he says, winking.

I don't understand if his comment is directed at me or our mutual comprehension of Chinese foreign relations.

"Anyway, it went well. You know trade, commerce, things like that. It was a long flight from China to Finland but having Air Force One does make it a lot more comfortable. We flew in pretty inconspicuously. Everyone in that little town was asleep by the time we landed. Still Air Force One is a large and recognizable plane to land in a small town like that, so we purposely leaked information to derail the media."

"What information?"

"We're in another country's air space, and obviously didn't want to cause a huge commotion or international crisis. We had the ambassador say we'd be visiting Scandinavia on some pressing business. I didn't want to get linked back to you. I believe the public thinks I'm either en route to Helsinki, or already there and fast asleep in the hotel."

When I don't respond, he asks, "How does President Meri feel about your presence here? I thought you two didn't get along?"

"He doesn't know."

Gosha's willowy figure hovers behind my back. A large wooden building breaks the monotony of conifers, nothing else surrounding it. A rectangular wooden box, the roof about to cave in, causes an uncomfortable feeling as we move in closer. The building's power emanates to Clinton, since he clenches his jaw. A scent wafts from the structure, the smell of a dead animal combined with eroding soil. I try to rearrange my face, to appear undisturbed, but its power seeps into my core.

"I think we've reached the old barracks," Clinton says.

He continues to walk toward the building. He motions to one of the security, who comes over and hands him an extra flashlight, which the president switches on and begins searching.

Trash overflows the building, but it's not regular rubbish. Yellowed newspapers are smudged with ink. A dirty, beheaded doll lies on the moss springing through the decaying floor. Her body contorts into an odd position while her head lies a meter away, the blonde curls matted with leaves. A rat's nest of synthetic hair. Clothing everywhere, bright reds, blues, greens. They're the clothes of small children. And shoes as well, little boots fit for a baby. Blue jeans, old textbooks, gloves. Their condition signals that someone or many people had dumped all this junk here somewhat recently. They're styles maybe of the 1980s, or the late 70s?

"Lots of junk," says Clinton.

"Yes."

"I guess it's the Estonian way of composting. Dump everything in the makeshift landfill. Well, I guess this place is as good as any. There's not much else you can do with it."

"Except tear it down."

"Well now, Vladimir, I would disagree. I wouldn't tear this place down."

"Why?"

"It represents their history. People suffered here."

"They use it as a landfill. They're not learning a history lesson from this place."

He shrugs. "You're probably right. I mean the outside isn't touched, but in here, it looks like a tornado hit."

I ask Gosha for an extra flashlight, which he hands me. I switch it on and focus on a corner. I walk closer to inspect. A bunk bed has been torn down, leaving a gash with crooked rusty nails jutting from the wall. As I shoot my light to the other corners, they have the same markings, the furious ripping off of bed frames. Meanwhile, Clinton crouches, forearms on his lower thighs, examining all the things on the floor. A musty smell intensifies the longer we remain in the barracks.

"I'll wait for you outside."

What I perceive to be irritation flickers across his face. Then it's gone and replaced by a wide smile.

"I'm following you, Vladimir."

We walk along the path again, the heaviness draining out my body. My normal self returns, aware of the situation.

"Bill," I say, turning to him. "I'd like to discuss the Moscow situation."

"Of course."

I clear my throat. I hadn't prepared a speech so this would be impromptu. He would probably cut right through any falsities anyway, so I speak the truth as best I can.

"I serve the Russian people, and now they've turned on me. The oligarchs vilify me in the media, adding to the tense situation."

Clinton nods.

"From the news reports, protests have spread to St. Petersburg and to some of the other cities. The outlook is not favorable for me, there's a chance of me losing the presidency. The longer I stay in hiding, the better the chance. I'd like to return to Moscow after this meeting."

"What do you need from me?"

"I know the oligarchs are friends of the Americans. I know you do business dealings with them. They have to back down."

Clinton stops walking. "Are you asking for my help?"

I stop. "I'm asking you to help the Russian people. They will suffer if the oligarchs seize power. The chaos will only continue to spread."

He walks. "Well, maybe. Or maybe you're not the right president for Russia?"

My face burns. "Who are you to decide that?"

He laughs. "Whoa, Vladimir. I didn't mean to insult you. I'm playing devil's advocate."

Gosha stumbles over the words, giving me a strange translation.

"What is this 'devil advocate'? An evil lawyer? What are you trying to say?"

"Never mind. Are you sure you want to remain president? I've been doing it for eight years and let me tell you, I'm exhausted. I'm worn out, my wife hates me and I have a shitty reputation."

"I sympathize with your situation, but the Russian people need me. They voted for me to be their president and I continue to serve them."

"Okay. Then you have to do something for me."

"What's that?"

"Save your sailors."

Deeper in the Forest

I'm in shock. I knew we'd talk about the Moscow situation, but the *Kursk*?

I halt and turn to him. "The sailors?"

Clinton stops and faces me.

"Yes, the *Kursk*."

"And this is why you came?"

"You look unfeeling, Vladimir. Uncaring, unsympathetic. Those sailors dying down there—it looks downright inhumane. Look, I'm sure you have your reasons, but indecision is the worst thing you can do. The Western media is tearing you apart as we speak. No matter the expense, the time, the manpower, you have to save those sailors. Otherwise, I can't help you. I'll be in deeper shit than I already am with the American people."

He says it like it's the easiest thing to do, as if digging for clams in the ocean.

"You must accept international aid. The Russian people want you to save their boys."

I say nothing.

"You have to do it today."

I stare straight ahead.

"You have no choice, Vladimir. If you do this, the protests and the oligarch problem will go away."

"Because of your influence?"

"No, because of you. The Russian people will see a human, not a KGB agent."

The horizon sizzles with a scarlet flame. A red hue peeks through the tree branches. Clinton looks to the morning sky. Gosha stands still.

I never listen to what the West says about us. Russia is always wrong, always evil. When I succeeded Yeltsin, I'd read a *New York Times* article that basically asked "Who is Vladimir Putin?" and then detailed my KGB past. That's what the Americans think of me. Only a few months into the presidency, I've grown accustomed to the bad press from the West, but these sailors, they do something to people. They spark an emotion, even in Russians. Our soldiers in Chechnya do not have the same effect. They die and everyone accepts it, but the sailors down there, in the ocean…

Enough!

Being viewed as cold and heartless, I can accept that, but accepting aid from the West is a humiliation.

"Thank you, Bill, but my experts are handling the situation. We have everything under control."

"You don't have *anything* under control. The US has the divers and the equipment, so does the UK and Norway. We can help you."

"What if the sailors are dead? Then it's a wasted mission. Wasted time and money."

"But at least you tried."

"Russia isn't the US. We don't waste money and resources."

He puts his hand on my shoulder. "The Russian people are speaking. They have a voice, whether you like it or not. Their voices are on the television and radio and in the newspapers. They want their leader to react. You've been silent for nearly four days. It's time to react."

I shrug off his hand.

"That's a real shame because your people need you. Think of your father, imagine him, down there in that sub suffocating minute by minute. It's an inhumane way to die. And we're talking about innocent boys who haven't even seen combat."

I look him straight in the eyes. "That's my decision."

"That's too bad, Vladimir. That's too bad."

A War Story

Clinton and his agents left a couple hours ago. I sit on this tree stump, my head in my hands. I have to return to the hideout and get my daughter, but I'm not ready to go back yet. I don't know what to do or where to go. Or who to turn to, except for Gosha or my family. A breeze pushes against my face.

I feel alone and powerless and tired. Very tired. My body feels heavy on this tree stump. The forest surrounds me as I sit in this clearing, a field of grass without any signs of a German past. The sunlight warms my exposed skin. A bird flies by. I look into the sky to watch it until it's a speck. Then I hear a rustling coming from the forest.

Gosha has already summoned my secret service, who stands with guns perched. I get up. This could be bad—it could be an Estonian policeman or military official who has received word of my being here. My meeting with Clinton took place so deep in the dense forest, I had doubted anyone had seen. I assumed the meeting spot was kilometers away from residential housing.

A man appears, hobbling. He's enormous. Is it Roman Kolesnikov again? I squint. No, Roman is fat and mildly tall; this man is huge and old. Crutches support him. My secret service inspects him. Gosha looks back to me as I walk towards them. The closer I get, the more familiar the man looks.

"Gospodin Putin, it's good to see you again."

It's the tour guide, the man I rescued out of the rubble.

"I'm Gennady Anatolovich, the tour—"

"Yes, I know who you are."

I signal to my secret service that he's fine. Gosha gapes at him.

He has a bandage from his brow bone to his nose. He hunches over his crutches. A wool cap sits atop his head.

I move closer and say, "Would you like to sit with me?"

He smiles and says, "Yes, Gospodin Putin, it would be my honor."

I tell Gosha to wait with security as we walk back to the tree stump. I sit on the ground and give him the stump. He sits down with a thud and lets out a groan.

"If I was twenty, I'd be recovered by now. A few shots of vodka and I'd be good. But now I'm an old man."

"What are you doing in this forest, Gennady Anatolovich? I thought the houses were kilometers away."

"Normally yes. The houses are far away. But I have a cottage close to here. Most people don't want to build where an old concentration camp was, but I don't mind. I lived in the forest for years, nothing bothers me anymore. Anyway, as I was falling asleep last night, hopped up on painkillers, I thought I heard voices, but I was too tired to stay awake. This morning I woke up and walked here to check everything out."

"I see."

He clears his throat. "Gospodin Putin, I, of course, won't ask what you're doing here nor will I say anything to anyone. You have my word."

I nod. "How are you feeling?"

"Okay, not so good. I've survived worse. Can't say the same for the Narva Castle. It's destroyed. You know, it was a big earthquake for us, measured 4.2 on the Richter scale."

"Do they know the cause?"

"Not yet."

He turns back to the view of conifers in front of him. I look at his flannel shirt, jeans and bandaged ankle and foot. He said he lived in the forest for years. This could be my last chance.

"Were you a forest brother, Gennady Anatolovich?"

He nods.

"For how many years did you live in the forest?"

"Seven."

"You're Estonian then?"

"I'm half Estonian, half Russian. My mother is from a small village in the south called Otepää. My father is from St. Petersburg."

"And you fought against the Soviets in the war?"

"Yes, the Soviets and the Nazis. I was loyal to the land, not any group. You have to realize back then, as a half Russian living in Narva, my family faced extreme prejudice. The Estonians hated us. Russians were a rare minority back then—the opposite of what Narva is today. I didn't want to side with the Soviets or the Nazis, so I chose the land."

"Did you ever meet any Soviets in the forest?"

"Yes."

"Did you help them?"

"I killed them."

I nod, refusing to show disappointment.

"Except for one."

His face becomes serious.

"Tell me about him."

The air was thick with blood. The sanguine fluid embedded in the dirt, on the drying autumn leaves, on the skin of the men in the forest. Always on the skin. Not a day went by without a scrape or cut or gunshot wound bursting through sinews. The sharp stings of salvo fire caused blood to spurt onto the bark of trees, seeping into their thousand-of-year-old rings. When the person would die, his blood spilled onto the earth, the roots of plants and trees drinking it all, mistaking it for nutrients. In 1944 the forest sprouted from the blood of the people living there, the Estonians who could not live in their society. They had pistols, machine guns, knives, grenades. Anything to fight off the enemy.

A Soviet wandered through the copse, or what he assumed was a copse. He found out it was a large forest. And he was alone. Most of his group blew up in front of his eyes. The skin taken right off his commander after the bomb; the charred man wasn't recognizable, lying dead on the ground. He didn't have time to look at the others so he ran into the forest and never looked back. The beauty of war was the silence after the bombing, the feeling that the enemy had retreated and you were safe at least for the moment.

So he wandered for days on end. Stumbling around the dense brush, his body bruised and aching. His head angled toward the ground, in search of mushrooms to eat. He was starving. This fungus grew wild in the forest, but apparently, other soldiers had gotten to them first. Delirium took over. He snatched dry leaves off the trees, crushed them in his hand and ate them like crumbs one by one. He fell asleep for the first three nights, tucked in ball, gun at his side, nibbling on leaves. He shivered as late autumn set into the countryside. Late autumn in Estonia meant snow. It would start snowing any day now—he could smell it in the air.

One morning he awoke with a shadow cast over him. He opened his eyes, expecting a large black cloud and snow to be melting onto his face. But instead, the shadow was a group of young men with guns pointed at his head. There were five of them, very young, maybe teenagers, but their faces were stern. They'd been out in the forest a while, the Soviet could tell. One pursed his lips together, made a disgusting sound with his throat and spat on the breast of the Soviet's uniform. The saliva hit in a glob and ran down his medals and pocket, absorbing into the fabric.

"Soviet cocksucker!" said the first soldier, kicking him in the thigh.

"How should we kill him? We can burn him with the leaves or send him to the concentration camp. They'll take care of him in there," another one said with a smirk on his face.

These men spoke flawless Russian. They had to be Estonians. He'd heard rumors of these people living in the forest. He never believed it because he hadn't run across them before.

"Take out his organs or burn him alive. He'll beg for mercy. Let's watch him beg for mercy."

Amongst themselves they started to debate over his life, but in Estonian. He lost all meaning of the conversation. The men still had their guns pointed at him, ready to fire. They weren't distracted. The Soviet knew he had nowhere to flee. As of this moment, he was an official prisoner of war. A humiliating POW because the main enemy, the Nazis, didn't capture him; instead this group of young Estonian vagabonds did.

"Get up!"

He struggled to his feet due to starvation, but it was too slow for the one man. He took his pistol and whipped him across the face and shouted, "Faster!"

He pushed himself off the dirt until one man reached forward and grabbed him, standing him up in one pull. Then he held him by the shoulder and reached his fist all the way back.

The Russian knew what was coming and shut his eyes. Knuckles collided into cheekbone. A good right hook. Pain interrupted his sense of gravity and he dropped to the ground as the other men broke into hysterics.

"We're kind! In the gulag, your people torture and maim."

The man kicked him in the head, sending the Soviet face first into the dirt, and then said, "I can't even look at this piglet. Soviet piglet."

"Don't kill him, Taivo, take it easy. We want to torture him first before he dies."

A few others laughed.

"Sorry, I can't help myself."

After one more blow to the head with a heavy boot, he was knocked unconscious. He didn't remember these men dragging his body through the dirt and mud as he smacked against tree trunks and rocks. He awoke at a campsite with a body full of bruises and reeking of urine. Either he pissed himself or they pissed all over him, most likely the latter. The smell radiated from his head. He started to reach up with one hand, but realized he was tied to a tree trunk, in sitting position. Only his head and legs weren't tied. They tied his arms and from his shoulders to his waist. The men hovered around the campfire, kneeling and warming their hands. They spoke in Estonian again, so he couldn't understand.

"Soup is ready," announced one man.

They each scooped the contents from a huge vat and passed bowls down the line. A young man, huge in stature, took a second bowl for himself.

"What are you doing?"

"He needs to eat."

"You're wasting our food on a Soviet?!"

"Mart, calm down. He needs to eat a little. Just half a serving."

"I knew it! You're just like them! Half-breed!" screamed Mart, dropping his bowl, about to charge the young man.

"*Rahulik*! Calm!" said Taivo, rushing over to Mart and grabbing him.

The Soviet thought the huge man wanted extra soup for himself.

"Take the soup and give him half a serving. I'm only agreeing so we keep him alive enough to send him over to the German camp. Tomorrow, the Soviet is gone; he's causing us too many problems."

"No, the kid is the problem."

"Genya," said Taivo, constraining Mart in a restrictive bear hug, "taking the motherfucking soup and feed it to him. No untying. And smell the piss on his head while you're doing it."

The boy took the bowl and a spoon and walked over to the half-unconscious Soviet. He kneeled down in front of him, dipping the spoon in the broth and holding it up to the Soviet's mouth. He thought it was poison and turned his face away.

"It's not poison," said Genya in Russian. "I'm not poisoning you. You've suffered enough. Have something to eat."

He opened his mouth, letting the mushroom soup fill his taste buds. Hot and watered down, plump mushrooms, maybe an onion...that was where all the mushrooms in the forest had gone. The liquid passed down his throat. He chewed the fungi slowly, on the side of his mouth that wasn't punched. The pain was excruciating.

Through chewing, he asked, "Who are you?"

Dipping the spoon into the bowl, Genya replied, "No. No names. I don't want to know your name especially when tomorrow comes. Leaving you at that concentration camp, I don't want that on my conscience. I don't want a name with a face."

He finished the bowl in silence, filling his minute appetite, his stomach shrunk to the size of a bullet. He wished he could ask the young man for a cold thing to put on his cheek, but the others would protest. The kid might get hurt. Nodding his thank you, he leaned his head back against the trunk. Eyes closed, he listened to a language of which he couldn't understand a word.

"His cheek is pretty bad," said Genya, back in the circle, hovering over the fire.

"Once a Russian—"

"Shut up, Mart! The kid is fine. His father is from Piter and he's a good man. Treated my father well at the factory."

"His father did what he was told by the other Russians. Look at him now. When Kreenholm is up and running, he's king. While all of our parents are out of work. What a good little Russian, huh?"

Mart reached over and patted Genya's head, making him flinch.

"At least Genya knows when to shut up. Your mouth is always going."

"The man's cheek is bad."

Taivo looked over at him, his blue eyes set on fire by the flames' illumination. "Fine Genya, take him something cold. A waste of time though, he'll just suffer more tomorrow."

He got up and searched for a cold, smooth object by the firelight until he found a rock.

Putting it against the Soviet's cheek, the man did not cry out in pain. Genya checked his neck for a pulse. It was there, thumping and warm. He held the stone against his face, the man in an unconscious state yet again. Sending him to the Nazis like this was not an option. They would do those horrible things that he had seen with his own eyes from the protection of the forest. He'd hear the man's tortuous screams all the way from Vaivara.

Snores erupted from the Soviet as Genya thought of a way to set him free. Satisfied, he took the rock off the man's face and walked back to the fire to keep warm.

The following morning had a brisk chill in the air. Winter announced itself with fledging flakes drifting from the grey sky. Genya covered his neck with a wool scarf, knitted by his mother ages ago for his twelfth birthday. He pulled the fur cap down over his face and grabbed his gun and walked over to Taivo.

As he stuffed things into his pack, Taivo looked up and said, "What?"

"I'll drop him off at the camp. It's too far out of everyone's way. We were heading west and now we'll have to go back east. Mart is already angry."

Taivo laughed. "I don't trust you to do that. You'll release him, the soft-hearted Russian you are."

"If you ever see him again, I will leave the group, leave the forest. And I'll leave Estonia for good, I promise you that. I will drop him off at the Vaivara gates."

"No, I want to see you do it with my own eyes."

"I will do it, Taivo. I don't want to put the group in anymore danger. If anything happens to one of you, if the Germans catch any of us, I'll be held responsible. Let me do it. You and the others continue west. I'll catch up."

The voice sounded more confident than the nineteen-year-old man Genya was. Before Taivo's eyes, he'd grown up, a child begging him for food, now ready to face the Nazis and risk his life for a stranger. He thought of him like a little brother. As naïve and idealistic the boy could be at times, he loved him.

"So now you're loyal to the Soviets," said Taivo, back to shoving food-stuffs in his pack.

"I'm not loyal to anyone. How can I be? I don't fit in anywhere. As I told you when this all began, I'm loyal to the land, that's it. Tell the others whatever you want, I'm taking the man."

Genya turned around and walked away toward the Soviet tied up around the tree.

"Hey Genya."

"Yeah?"

"I know you're going to set him free. Don't let me see him again. I will keep you to your promise."

"I won't—"

Taivo put up his hand. "Don't lie to me. Go now while the others are gathering mushrooms and water."

"Thank you."

Taivo shook his head and kept on packing.

The gates loomed, hidden by the canopy of trees. Guards paced back and forth. Prisoners hovered at the wire fence. Genya and the Soviet remained at a safe distance. Genya had observed the Germans' strict schedule months ago; he knew they didn't waver from it.

He whispered in the Soviet's ear, "That could be you. In the distance, behind that fence. I'm going to send you out there in this uniform."

The man trembled. "Please, please don't. I have a wife, I have par—"

"Shut up!" the boy hissed. "Shut up! I'm in enough trouble because of you. I should kill you."

Aware that these would be his last few days alive, he dropped down to his knees and said, "Fine, kill me then. It's better than what I'll get in there."

"Get up!"

Genya grabbed the man by the shoulder and pulled him off the ground, standing him straight. He could feel the man shudder in his palm.

"Go east. Walk until you get to the border. Don't come back or I will kill you, and I know this forest better than you ever will. Don't pull any tricks. Go."

The boy gave the Russian a great shove and then ran off. The Soviet fell to the ground, catching himself with his hands at the last moment. He looked back. The boy was already gone. And he was alone.

"That's it, Gospodin Putin. That's all I know about that Soviet. He caused me so much trouble, I didn't help anyone again. Kept to myself and killed when it was necessary."

I look into the grass. That Soviet could've been my father. He could have. If only Gennady Anatolovich had asked for his name.

"Are you trying to find out about a particular Soviet soldier, Gospodin Putin?"

"Yes."

"If I may ask, who?"

"My father."

"Ah. Is that why you came to Narva in the first place?"

Why do I feel so comfortable confiding in this stranger, who is half Estonian?

"My father said Estonians saved him during the war. It was cryptic. I have no other information."

The weight of exhaustion sets in and tugs on my brain. I can't think or talk anymore.

As I stand up, I say, "Gennady Anatolovich, I have to go. I trust that you've given me your word."

"Of course, Gospodin Putin. I owe you for saving my life."

I nod and walk toward Gosha and my security, leaving the old tour guide sitting on the tree stump.

Dream

I drift off to sleep quickly, but a disturbing dream haunts me. It consists of a stormy sea, the current raging. I stand alone on a beach on an unfamiliar shoreline, not the one at my dacha in Sochi or in the Greek islands. In the pitch black, a large figure walks toward me from across the way. Cold, I pull my winter jacket closer and wait for the man to approach. Now I can see by the light of the moon it's Gennady Anatolovich, who's barefoot, his enormous feet imprinting the wet sand like an abominable snowman. Without fear, he stands right in front of me, towering over my cold, wet frame. Then he looks away, out to the sea, and points.

In the middle of the waves, an arm extends vertically. The hand curls its fingers up and down, performing an eerie wave. The moonlight shines upon a gold band that wraps around its wedding ring finger. It has an insignia. I don't understand how I can read the letters from kilometers away but I can. Instantly, the scene pans into the ring's engraving. It says: *For you. For all of us. Help.* When I reach out to grab the ring and pull it off the finger, the arm sinks beneath the waves. I dive into the water and open my eyes, which sting from the salt. A woman swims away from me, her arms peacefully stroking. She glides downwards, her legs flapping back and forth like a fish. She is natural to the water and I struggle to match her pace. I follow, wondering how I'm able to breathe underwater for such a long time.

We swim and swim, moving through the deep abyss, a lantern fish lighting the way every once in a while. Even though I should be terrified, I'm not. I follow her, soon passing underneath a giant blue whale. I reach out and touch the smooth surface, grazing my hand along the entire length of its stomach. But the whale swims away and the chasm becomes deeper and blacker, frightening me that I will never return home.

The woman reaches what appears to be the ocean floor as she touches the sand but keeps swimming. She drifts until she bounces back. She tries to swim again, stroking more powerfully with her arms and pumping her legs, but she keeps hitting something and bouncing back. It goes on like this until I catch up to her. At that point, she's hysterical, pushing and bouncing. When I tap the woman's shoulder, only then she stops and paddles aside for me to try. With all my physical and mental strength, I propel forward, smacking head first into a clear wall. We're in some type of tank.

The air in my lungs begins to dissipate. An imaginary force strangles me. I can't breathe. I gasp for air, my hands curled around my throat.

The morning comes too soon. For a moment, I forget where I am, a habit from traveling so often. My fingers ache from curling them in my sleep and my throat is dry from the imaginary salt water I had ingested in the dream.

I wipe the crust from my eyes and the sides of my mouth. I sit up, remembering where I am and my situation. The dream. The ring. The insignia. I felt strangulation, the air rushing out of my lungs. I shudder. Usually, I don't remember my dreams, but this one was vivid. Too vivid. And too real.

No sun or windows in this tiny bedroom, I'm lying in a crypt. The protests. The sailors. My wife and Katya in Berlin. Masha trapped here with me. Three months into my presidency and I've created a mess that even I don't know how to get out of. I couldn't use my old KGB skills to divert attention. I couldn't blame it on Yeltsin. I misjudged everything from the logistics of the *Kursk* to the reaction of the Russian people to the power of the oligarch-led media. I could continue to run or I could choose help.

I push the comforter away and jump out of bed. I look down at myself, realizing I had fallen asleep in my work clothes. I rush to the door and open it.

"Gosha, get in here."

He drops his mobile on the kitchen table and comes in. I shut the door. "Where's Masha?"

"She's outside with a guard. She wanted some fresh air."

"Call Secretary Albright. Tell Clinton I'm accepting international aid from whoever is offering."

Gosha smiles but stops once he sees my expression.

"And tell secret service we're heading back to the Kremlin. Now."

No Turning Back

Masha and Gosha ride together in a separate car in my motorcade. I need to ride alone to allow myself time to think. The driver speeds through the back roads and then on the highways. He seems anxious to get home as well. Trees flash by, the provinces, the exact same as when I had left. It seems like nothing has changed, but it actually has. I dressed like a president this morning, as I wear a suit, tie and my favorite Prada loafers.

Having Gosha make the phone call was not easy, but after I did, a sense of calm flooded over me. I knew I was back in. The next call I received was from Oleg Petrovich, my old KGB supervisor, who gathered former agents to round up the oligarchs and force them out of Moscow. He said for the time being they forced Khodorkovsky all the way to Greece.

"Thank you, Oleg Petrovich."

"You're welcome, Gospodin Putin. We're here to serve you, but we need your help."

I understood the underlying meaning. It was time to put the right people in power, get rid of Yeltsin's useless staff, including Sergeyev who hadn't helped at all.

I won't lose power again.

I've learned my lessons. The times I'd let my guard down were the times I'd failed throughout my life. The judo match against the girl. Believing the *Kursk* was indestructible. And what had just happened, believing the people would support me in any crisis. I followed my security like an obedient dog, when it should've been the other way around. Before leaving my house, I should've questioned my security, called Oleg Petrovich to confirm the situation and never left the capital. But I've learned my lesson. I will never be weak again. I will never follow again.

I will return to my roots, to my KGB discipline and to judo. I will live by my mantra. "Greatness lies not in being strong, but in the right use of strength."

My wife and daughter are flying back from Germany as I sit here. They are safe. Lyuda even told me that it was almost a vacation, as she caught up with the Chancellor's wife and visited their country house.

I made security provide me with a mobile. On the screen I can see it's Sergeyev calling, so I let it ring.

News

On the other line, Sergeyev listens to the unanswered ring, wishing Putin would pick up. They've found out more news about the *Kursk*, about the second explosion. Its power was equivalent to nearly three tons of TNT, or almost seven warheads, causing a surprise earthquake that was felt in Northern Europe.

Gosha and Masha

They've remained silent the entire ride, but in this last hour, Masha began to talk. She has the sudden urge to speak to Gosha.

"How do you like working for my father?"

She interrupts his reverie. Tanya, his little sister, called a few minutes ago to say the car broke down again. This time on the way to her job. The muffler sputtered and fell off. As she told him all this information, he replied, "okay," because he didn't want Masha to know it was a personal call and report back to Putin.

Masha asks once more. "How do you like working for my father?"

"It's fine. I like my job."

"Is he nice to you?"

"Yes."

"Then why do I see you hiding when you eat in the kitchen? Papa won't let you eat our food, will he?"

Gosha chooses not to respond.

"Katya sees you stealing our food too. We don't care if you eat it. You're skinny, so you can't be eating much."

Masha fiddles with the headphones to her music player. "I'm bored."

"You'll be home soon, Mariya Vladimirovna."

"This trip was such a waste. We shouldn't have left Moscow in the first place."

Gosha agrees in silence.

She says, "It won't happen again."

"I hope so."

"Papa won't let it."

Goodbye

The pen drops from the Lieutenant Captain's hand and pings on the steel floor. The head rolls to one side and stops. The body slides down the wall and collapses. Through closed eyelids, Dima sees the dark with colored specks interspersed. They fade away as white circles full of bloody veins float in his vision. Then the circles disappear and the drip-drip of the hull goes silent. The blood does not pump, the heart does not beat. A young woman in Vidyayevo is now a widow.

BACK TO THE PRESENT
June 2012

"You can stop recording," Putin says.

Gosha hits STOP on the mobile.

"We're finished."

"Yes, Gospodin Putin."

Gosha starts to rise from the chair.

"You can send it to the editors. I gave them the story they wanted. But I decide on what gets published."

"Yes, Gospodin Putin. They know."

"Remind them again."

"Of course."

Gosha grabs his suit jacket and walks out the door. Another twelve years of working for Putin. Can he do it? His shoes scuffle across Red Square, as he passes a small anti-Putin protest that the FSB is breaking up. It's late, midnight, but these ongoing protests have been growing more popular. Gosha wonders if it's young people expressing their opinions or real protesters starting a national movement against too many years of one president. He's not sure.

Tonight he's excited because the memoir is done and because he's meeting Tanya and Arkady at the GUM café to discuss their upcoming wedding. It will be a small affair, which Gosha hopes to attend if he can get the day off work.

As he approaches the café, he stops in Red Square and looks into the evening sky. He misses his hometown of Piter, which has White Nights now, the pink and violet clouds floating across the blue horizon at midnight. It would look like an early summer evening. When Mama had spare money, the family would take a boat packed with tourists and sail on the canals of the Neva River. The golden lights of the Hermitage would shine and Tanya would claim they were fairies holding up their wands.

Gosha smiles to himself. Nights like this made life okay. Whether he has a job for the next twelve years or doesn't, he could always return home. Return to his childhood apartment and live with Tanya and Arkady. The future remains uncertain for both Gosha and his boss, but whatever happens, at least there's a wedding to look forward to.

http://vladimirputinnovel.com/

Made in the USA
Lexington, KY
29 October 2013